The Christmas Tin
II

by Roderick J. Robison

ISBN-13: 978-0692514979
ISBN-10: 069251497X

For Leidimar

Prologue

December 24, 2010

I did not see Anna when she stepped into the living room this morning. I was installing an oak mantel above the fireplace at the time and was immersed in my work. It was when I turned around to reach for a level in my toolbox that I saw her.

Anna was standing in front of the bay window. She was sipping coffee. My daughter's eyes were focused on the old Christmas Tin on the bay windowsill.

Most people wouldn't give the old tin a second look. The metal is tarnished, and the hand-painted holly leaves and red berries on the tin's lid faded long ago. There are a number of nicks and scratches on both the tin and its lid.

Anna seemed lost in thought. I wondered if she was reflecting back to the day I first told her the story of the Christmas Tin. Anna was ten years old at the time.

There had been a quizzical expression on her face the day she inquired about the Christmas Tin. "Was it Grandma or Grandpa's?" Anna had asked.

"No, honey," I answered. "The Christmas Tin didn't belong to anyone in the family. It was given to me by someone very special a long time ago."

1

Anna's eyebrows lifted as I informed her that the Christmas Tin had been bequeathed to me by an elderly woman I delivered papers to during a holiday season back in my youth. The woman's name was Ardella Calder.

That holiday season—December 1968—had not been filled with much joy for my mother and me. My father was serving a tour of duty in Vietnam; my mother and I worried about him constantly. We were struggling to make ends meet, and I had given little thought to Christmas.

It was during that time that I first saw the Christmas Tin. It was resting on the windowsill in Ardella's room at the Beldon Manor Nursing Home. When I delivered her paper that day, Ardella saw me looking at the tin. My interest was not lost on her. She informed me that she stored gifts and mementos from some of her most memorable Christmases inside the tin.

That December, Ardella told me the story of the Christmas Tin. And she told me heartwarming stories behind each of the items inside the tin. I found solace in Ardella's stories. The stories provided a much needed reprieve from my constant worries.

Then just before Christmas, we received a telegram and learned that my father was MIA. It was the darkest period of my life. Upon hearing the dire news about my father, Ardella shared a final story with me, a poignant wartime holiday story. A story that guided me through my grief and showed me that faith and hope can sometimes bring light to even the darkest of places.

In the years that followed, my family continued the tradition of the Christmas Tin. We placed mementos from our most memorable Christmases in the tin.

The day I first told Anna the story of the Christmas Tin, she placed her own memento in the tin—a picture she had taken with her first Polaroid. It was a picture of my mother and me standing in front of a Christmas tree.

A decade has passed since I first told Anna the story of the Christmas Tin. Anna is twenty years old now and home from college for Christmas break. She spent the previous year studying in England. Anna had not able to make it home for Christmas last year.

How glad we were to have her home for the holidays this year. My wife, Mariana, and I picked her up at the bus station last night.

"Hi, sweetheart."

Anna smiled and shifted her focus to me. "Hey, Dad. I didn't want to interrupt you. It looked like you were engrossed in your work."

"Thanks for the thought, but you can interrupt me anytime."

"I'll keep that in mind."

"We saved some decorating for you," I said, gesturing to a box of ornaments beside the Christmas tree. Like her mother, Anna loved to decorate the Christmas tree.

"Thanks, Dad. I've been looking forward to it."

"I know."

The phone rang just then. "Be right back," I said. "Hopefully it's the lumber yard with news about the wainscoting I ordered." I had been on a home improvement kick as of late.

When I returned to the living room five minutes later, Anna was sitting on the couch. The Christmas Tin was no longer on the bay windowsill. Anna had placed it on the coffee table in front of the couch. She removed the Christmas Tin's lid as I stepped into the room.

3

Anna's eyes widened as she peered into the Christmas Tin. "There are new things inside the tin!" she exclaimed. "What did I miss out on last Christmas?!"

I couldn't help but smile. Anna lived for the holidays as much as I did. She loved Christmas. I knew it must have been tough on her being so far away from the family last December.

"Well, I said. "Last Christmas was...different."

"Oh?"

"I didn't have much Christmas spirit going into the holiday season last year," I stated.

Anna gasped. "You're kidding, right?" My daughter knew well my fondness for the holidays. I was known to bring the boxes of Christmas decorations down from the attic the day after Thanksgiving.

I shook my head. "I was a bit distracted last holiday season. I guess I didn't mention my *situation* last year."

Anna furrowed her brow in concern. "No, Dad. You didn't."

"Did Mom mention anything to you about it?"

Anna shook her head. "She did not."

I nodded. "Mom probably didn't want to distract you from your studies. Neither did I."

Anna's eyebrows arched. "Dad, you're worrying me now. You have my attention. Did you have a health issue?"

"No, sweetheart. I'm healthy as can be. Ran five miles yesterday."

"That's a relief. Well, what was the *situation* you alluded to? Do tell."

I unbuckled my toolbelt and placed it on top of the newly-installed oak mantel. "Tell you what. Let's get some of those cranberry muffins

4

your mother made this morning and freshen up your coffee. Then I'll tell you all about it."

Five minutes later we were seated on the living room couch sipping coffee. A plate of cranberry muffins rested on the coffee table beside the Christmas Tin. It was just the two us in the house. Anna's brother, Paul, was at swim practice; Mariana was working. The house was unusually quiet.

Anna gave me a questioning look.

"Okay, okay," I smiled. I took a long pull of coffee from my mug and placed the mug on the coffee table. "Do you have some time?" I asked. "It's not a quick story."

Anna leaned back into the couch. "Dad, time is something I have plenty of at this moment."

"Okay then."

I drifted back to the previous autumn…

Chapter 1

September 29, 2009

I was sitting at my desk, immersed in an income and expense report when Wendy knocked on the door to my office. I liked Wendy. She was always upbeat. Wendy was a single parent, had a four-year-old daughter who meant the world to her.

"Giuseppe Moretti is on line two," she said. "He'd like to talk to you."

I winced. It wasn't that I disliked the man. On the contrary, I respected and admired Giuseppe Moretti, had always enjoyed talking with him.

I had met Giuseppe Moretti two years earlier at a real estate conference. The man owned a modest portfolio of properties that he self-managed. He called me for advice now and then.

Giuseppe Moretti moved to America when he was twelve years old. His father was a mason. Giuseppe learned the trade from his father. He saved nearly every cent he made his first ten years in America.

The man invested in a two-family dwelling on the outskirts of Beldon when he was 22 years old. A few years later, using the equity from his first investment, he invested in a rundown six-unit apartment complex and renovated it during weekends and evenings after punching out at his day job.

Giuseppi Moretti continued to acquire properties in the years that followed. He bought additional multi-family dwellings, small apartment complexes, a medium-sized strip mall, and most recently, an eighteen-unit townhouse complex. All of his properties were within a thirty-mile radius of the small western Massachusetts town of Beldon. I suspected his call was related to his most recent acquisition.

Aside from being an astute real estate investor, Giuseppe Moretti was a gentle, kind-hearted family man, probably a decade younger than my grandfather. And he liked to talk. Giuseppe always asked about my family before revealing the purpose of his call. Any other day I'd welcome the chance to talk with him. But I had a meeting in ten minutes with my boss—the owner of Berkshire Hills Property Associates, Inc., and I was busy preparing for the meeting.

"Please tell Giuseppe I'm not available right now," I told Wendy. "I'll get back to him."

"You got it, boss."

I had worked for Berkshire Hills Property Associates, Inc. for eight years. Prior to that, I had been a correspondent, spending more time overseas than at home. I had missed out on so much during my years as a correspondent. I was not there for birthdays, countless holidays, and many family get-togethers. Hence my career change.

Changing careers had been challenging at the time—to say the least. I had no previous real estate experience, short of the summers I worked on framing crews and construction sites during high school and college. Obtaining a Certified Property Manager (CPM) designation had been particularly challenging as my correspondent job often kept me on the road. I attended the required courses during vacation time over a three-

8

year period, forgoing precious family time. But the sacrifice paid off when I was hired by Berkshire Hills Property Associates, Inc.

I began my employment with Berkshire Hills Property Associates as an onsite property manager for a moderate-sized residential apartment complex. Two years later I was promoted to the position of executive property manager.

Berkshire Hills Property Associates owned five apartment complexes ranging in size from 18-175 units. In addition to the property-owned portfolio, the firm managed three properties for investors—a 24-unit office building, a 32-unit apartment complex known as Beldon Gardens, and a strip mall. As executive property manager, I oversaw the management of all eight properties.

I held the position of executive property manager for nearly four years before being promoted to my current position. I was now the director of property management for the company.

Wendy stopped by my office five minutes later to let me know the meeting with my boss—Burt Simms—was cancelled. Wendy didn't know the reason for the cancellation.

A half hour later, I passed by the conference room on my way down the hall to fax a document. Burt Simms and the firm's attorney, Miles Kadlik, were seated at the conference room's rectangular table. Across the table from them were three men I had never seen before. All three were clad in suits and wingtips. Wendy shrugged her shoulders when I passed by her desk. She didn't know who the men were either.

My guess was that Burt and Miles were meeting with representatives from the firm's insurance company. The insurance policy was up for renewal soon, and Burt liked to handle insurance matters himself. It was obvious the five of them were not there to discuss an acquisition. I would have been invited to the meeting had that been the case. I didn't dwell on it. There was too much to do.

The remainder of my work day was consumed with lease negotiations, budgeting, and meetings with contractors and onsite managers. As I pulled out of the employee parking lot after work that evening, it occurred to me that I hadn't returned Giuseppe Moretti's call.

*****

I met my college roommate, Bill Thimpson, for a game of racquetball after work. We had a court reserved at the club for six-thirty. Bill was in the locker room when I arrived. The expression on his face indicated that his day had not been a good one. Bill worked in the software industry.

"Hey," I said, giving him a customary slap on the back.

"Hey, Jesse."

"Why the long face?"

"Well…I got laid off today," Bill said. "Again."

I winced. "Wow, sorry to hear that."

"Yeah, well, I'll bounce back. But it looks like I'll have to give up that new SUV I bought last month. Unemployment checks won't cover a car payment *and* the rent. Not if I want to eat."

"You know you can count on me if you need help," I said.

Bill managed a smile. "I know. I'll make it through this. Thanks though. Let's play some racquetball."

"You're on."

*****

On the drive home from the club later on, I reflected on Bill's situation. How lucky I was to have a secure, high-paying job. If I was in Bill's situation—laid off—I'd have a lot more to worry about than giving up an SUV. I had a significant mortgage, a daughter in college overseas, a son who would soon be in college, two car payments, and all of the usual utility and household bills.

How fortunate I was. I had a great compensation package, and I respected the man I worked for. My co-workers were good people too, and I enjoyed my work. Yes, I was lucky indeed. And I took it all for granted.

Chapter 2

I called Giuseppe Moretti's office when I arrived at work the following morning. Giuseppe's secretary informed me that he had left the country that morning. She told me that Giuseppe was vacationing in Italy, visiting family. He would be out of the country for a month.

Wendy knocked on the door to my office just after I hung up. She looked distraught. "Burt would like to meet with you in his office at nine o'clock."

I looked up from the paperwork on my desk. "Do you know the nature of the meeting?"

Wendy furrowed her brow. Then she stepped into my office and closed the door. "No, I don't. But remember those three *suits* in the conference room yesterday?"

"Yes."

"I saw them pull out of the parking lot in a black BMW after they met with Burt and Miles. The license plate read: CNE REG."

"As in Central New England Real Estate Group?"

Wendy nodded. "That's my guess."

Central New England Real Estate Group was a regional real estate management firm. They were much larger than Berkshire Hills Property Associates.

"Any clues as to what yesterday's meeting was about?" I inquired.

Wendy shook her head. "Your guess is as good as mine."

"Thanks, Wendy."

She smiled. "You bet. Keep me updated, boss."

"Will do."

I walked down the hall at nine o'clock and knocked on the door to Burt's office. It was half open. "Morning, Burt."

"Jesse. Come in, come in."

I stepped into Burt's office. Framed photographs of office buildings and apartment complexes were neatly aligned on the walls. Nestled between them were pictures of Burt's grandchildren and several diplomas.

Burt smiled and motioned to a leather-cushioned chair in front of his colossal mahogany desk. "Shut the door and have a seat, Jesse."

I shut the door and sat down in the chair in front of Burt's desk.

"Jesse, I'll get right to the point. I want you to be the first one in the office to know. I have decided to retire."

My eyebrows lifted. "Congratulations, Burt! That's great. You've worked hard. You certainly deserve it."

"Thanks, Jesse. I appreciate that. My wife and I will be moving to Florida. Bought a nice little home in a development in Sarasota. We've always enjoyed the area."

"Good for you," I said. "When do you plan to move?"

"Just over a month from now."

"Well, you know you don't need to worry about anything around here. I'll keep you updated on the properties, everything will run smoothly. How often do you plan to come back? Once a month or so?" There was no doubt that Burt would continue to be involved in the business he had spent half a lifetime building.

Burt winced. "The thing is, Jesse. I won't be coming back. I'm selling out. Selling the business and the portfolio...to Central New England Real Estate Group."

My heart raced. "...Central New England Real Estate Group?" I stammered.

"That's right. They have a fine reputation."

"...When is the closing?"

"Thirty days from now. October 30th."

"What about our *jobs*? Are they secure?"

Burt coughed. Then he said, "Central New England Real Estate Group is far larger than Berkshire Hills Property Associates. I'd think there would be a lot of potential for advancement there. They own and manage nearly 5,000 units."

"I'm familiar with the name," I said. I had met a few property managers from Central New England Real Estate Group at a conference a few years back.

"Central New England Real Estate Group has a significant portfolio in eastern Massachusetts, but they don't own or manage any property in the western part of the state," Burt said. "Hence their interest in the firm. They are quite eager to expand into Berkshire County."

"Burt, about our jobs. Will we be *working* for Central New England Real Estate Group? Are we going to be on their payroll?"

"Relax, Jesse. You have nothing to worry about. Central New England Real Estate Group informed me they have no immediate plans to make any changes. They will not be making any decisions until after an appropriate evaluation period. And with your work ethic and knowledge of the portfolio, you have no need to worry."

Could you put that in writing? "Well," I said, "If you need any help with the transition, just let me know. I'll do whatever I can to assist."

Burt flashed a smile. "I know. Thanks, Jesse. I'll be counting on your help."

*****

The next morning, the vice president of Central New England Real Estate Group and two of his regional managers visited the office. Burt and I spent two hours with them. I never get headaches, but that morning was an exception. My schedule, I learned, would be busier than ever in the weeks ahead.

The terms of the purchase and sale agreement mandated that Phase I Environmental Site Assessments be conducted for each property in the Berkshire Hills Property Associates portfolio. Any environmental issues that were uncovered would need to be addressed before the closing. I had a lot of work ahead of me.

*****

Every minute of each work day in the weeks that followed was filled with tasks. Between scheduling the Phase I Environmental Site Assessments and coordinating the testing of oil tanks, scheduling asbestos abatement and lead paint removal, and other environmental projects, it seemed there was never enough time during the work day. I often didn't return home until late at night.

Mariana did her best to allay my fear and apprehension during our later-than-usual dinners. She put a positive spin on the whole thing, telling me how good it was that I was already working with upper management at Central New England Real Estate Group, and how they would surely see what a hard worker I was. She pointed out that the environmental experience I was gaining would be beneficial to my career. Mariana was always upbeat. It was one of the things I loved about her. "Everything will be fine, *meu amor*," she told me. "You will see. And remember—we'll be sunning ourselves on the beach in Aruba, come February."

I finally managed a smile. "You'll be on the beach. I'll be fishing."

Our twentieth anniversary was coming up in February. We had decided to spend our anniversary in Aruba, a destination both of us had always wanted to visit.

Chapter 3

Friday, October 30

Wendy planned a retirement luncheon for Burt Simms. It was held at noon—four hours before the closing. The luncheon was held at Nick's Diner. Wendy and some of the office staff had gone to the diner before work that morning to decorate it with banners and balloons.

It was literally impossible for me to leave the office at noon. I was the last person to arrive at Burt's retirement luncheon. There must have been upwards of a hundred people crammed inside the diner. Everyone from the office was there, along with the maintenance staff, onsite managers and assistant managers from each of the apartment complexes. Also in attendance were contractors, members of the janitorial crew, and various friends. Miles Kadlik, the firm's attorney, was there too.

Burt had been a good boss. He'd always treated his employees fairly and paid them well. Burt gave Christmas bonuses in down years as well as up years. No matter the state of the economy, his employees could count on their Christmas bonus. Burt would be missed.

Burt was just finishing up his speech when I arrived. I caught the tail end of it: "Thank you all very much again for all of your help and dedication over the years. You have made the firm what it is today. I will be forever grateful to each and every one of you. Central New England Real Estate Group has a fine reputation, and I am sure each of you will prosper under their ownership. God bless."

Chapter 4

Monday, November 2

During the drive to work that morning I had a flashback to running track in high school. Before each race I had *butterflies*—an uneasiness that settles into your stomach when you're nervous. I hadn't run the 440 in years, but I had butterflies all the same.

Reginalde Kalhume, the vice president of Central New England Real Estate Group, had moved his belongings into Burt's former office over the weekend. He was on the phone at Burt's old mahogany desk when I passed by on the way down the hall to my office. His regional managers—Thomas and Davis—were in the conference room. Thomas was talking on his cell phone; Davis was punching keys on his laptop. Like Reginalde Kalhume, both of them were clad in suits and wingtips.

I was wearing my usual attire—an oxford shirt, a conservative tie, khaki pants and rubber-soled leather shoes. I made a mental note to wear a suit or at least a sport coat from now on. I'd have to pass on the wingtips, though. I had always been more of a hands on property manager; leather-soled wingtips didn't provide much traction on asphalt roofs or slippery boiler room floors.

I arrived at work an hour earlier than usual. Wendy wasn't in yet. I went into my office and listened to voicemail. Then I turned on my computer and checked my e-mail. I debated walking down the hall to knock on Reginalde's door to check in with him, but decided to hold off for the time being. I suspected he was still on the phone. Reginalde stepped into my office a few minutes later.

"Good morning, Jesse."

"Morning, Reginalde."

"We're meeting in the conference room in five minutes. You, myself, Thomas, and Davis."

"Sure. Be right down," I replied as Reginalde headed back to his office.

What a contrast. Burt had always asked how my weekend was before getting back to business on Monday morning. This guy was all business.

I walked down to the conference room a few minutes after Reginalde left. Reginalde, Thomas, and Davis were there. They were seated at the rectangular table. I immediately felt underdressed. The casual dress code days were gone.

"Hello, Jesse," Reginalde said. He gestured for me to take a seat. Davis got up and shut the door. Then he returned to his seat. Reginalde got right down to business.

"Jesse," he began, "now that the Phase I ESAs and environmental projects are behind us, the next step will be to familiarize Thomas and Davis with each property. They need to be familiar with each property in the Central New England Real Estate Group portfolio. You can learn a lot from them. I'm sure the three of you will work well together."

"I look forward to it," I said.

"Very good. I'd like the three of you to work together this week. Thomas and Davis will need to get out to each property and do a walk-through at each site. In addition to seeing the boiler rooms and all common areas, they'll need to see at least six units at each complex, preferably more. And they'll need to review all of the property files—maintenance agreements, management contracts, budgets, building plans, etc. They'll also need to review delinquency lists and rent rolls for each property."

I nodded. "No problem."

"Very well. We have a busy week ahead of us, gentlemen. This meeting is adjourned."

Thomas and Davis followed me down the hall to my office after the meeting. As with Reginalde Kalhume, there was no small talk with them. No chatting about the score of the Patriots game or the Bruins prospects.

The first things Thomas and Davis wanted to review were the management contracts for the three investor-owned properties. I pulled the management contracts from the file cabinet in my office and handed them over. Thomas and Davis took the management contracts down to the conference room. While they reviewed them, I called the onsite managers at the various apartment complexes and scheduled site visits.

Later that morning, I brought Thomas and Davis to the three investor-owned buildings. My thought was that visiting the investor-owned buildings first would provide the onsite managers at the larger apartment complexes more time to prepare for the site visits.

We swung by the 24 unit office building first. The owner of the building, Steve Hartnick, was an architect. Steve had an office on the second floor. We stopped by his office and I introduced him to Thomas and Davis and explained that Central New England Real Estate Group had acquired Berkshire Hills Property Associates.

I liked Steve. He was easy going and had always appreciated my efforts. All three investors did. They never haggled over annual management contract increases or needed repairs. The three of them were professionals, and they trusted me to get the job done.

Thomas and Davis took turns asking me questions throughout the tour. When did the commercial leases expire? How much was the rent per square foot? When was the last market analysis performed? How old was the roof? What was the age of the boiler? Thomas and Davis noted everything in their tablets.

After the tour of the office building we headed across town to Beldon Gardens, a 32 unit apartment complex owned by Jake Templeton. Thomas and Davis asked the same questions during our time there. It was as if they had rehearsed the questions. Jake happened to be there and I introduced him to Thomas and Davis before we left.

Next, we drove across town to the strip mall, the third investor-owned property. Ike Cauldwelle, the owner, was not onsite at the time. Once again, Thomas and Davis asked the same questions and noted the answers in their tablets.

We completed the third tour at noon. I mentioned that Nick's Diner was just down the road and told Thomas and Davis I'd be glad to join them for lunch.

"That's okay," Davis replied. "We're meeting a friend at a café across town. We'll meet back at the office at one o'clock."

"Okay, see you then."

*****

When Thomas and Davis returned to the office at one o'clock, I couldn't help but wonder if Reginalde was the "friend" who Davis had mentioned. Reginalde was right behind them. I was talking with Wendy in the reception area, checking messages, when the three of them walked by.

Thomas had to return to the corporate office in Boston that afternoon. Davis stepped into the conference room to peruse property files. Reginalde holed up in Burt's old office, and I spent the afternoon at my desk drafting lease agreements and talking to onsite managers.

Every ten minutes or so, Davis stopped by my office with a question. Had it been me, I would have written them down and compiled a list of questions that could be addressed in one sitting. These guys apparently operated under different rules.

The remainder of the week was spent visiting the rest of the properties in the Berkshire Hills Property Associates portfolio. I introduced Thomas and Davis to the onsite managers, assistant managers, and maintenance staff at each apartment complex.

I provided Thomas and Davis with comprehensive property information sheets for each complex, but that didn't stop their questions. They had many questions, and there was an underlying urgency in their tone. It seemed Thomas and Davis wanted to learn as much as they could about each property as quickly as possible. I had to give them credit for their perseverance—by the end of the day on Friday, the two of them we're basically up to speed on each property in the portfolio.

Wendy stopped by my office just before five o'clock on Friday afternoon to let me know that Giuseppe Moretti had called. She informed me that Giuseppe had recently returned from Italy. I picked up the phone and was about to call Giuseppe when Reginalde stepped into my office.

"Can you meet me in my office before you finish up?" he asked.

"Sure. Be right there."

I hung up the phone and headed down the hall to Burt's old office—Reginald's office. Wendy was on the phone when I passed by the reception desk. She cupped the receiver and said, "Have a good weekend. See you Monday."

"You, too. Thanks for all the help, as usual."

Reginalde Kalhume was seated behind Burt's mahogany desk when I stepped into his office. He was on the phone. Reginalde motioned to the leather-padded chair in front of the desk. I sat down. Everyone in the office had left by the time Reginalde finished the call. It was just the two us.

"Jesse," he said. "I want to thank you for your all of your help this week."

"My pleasure. Glad I could be of assistance."

"We've accomplished a lot this week. It seems Thomas and Davis now have a firm grasp on the portfolio…and that brings me to the reason I called you down to my office. Jesse, there's no easy way to say this. I'll get right to the point. Thomas and Davis will be assuming your responsibilities as of Monday."

My heart raced. "…Thomas and Davis are going to work *here*? Out of this office?"

Reginald shook his head. "No, they'll be based at corporate in Boston."

"…Do you have another position in mind for me?"

"No. I did look into another position for you, but there is nothing open right now... You are being laid off, I regret to say. But please know that I'll do anything I can to help you. If a position opens up, you'll be the first to know about it. And if you need a reference—"

"I've been with Berkshire Hills Property Associates for eight years," I cut in. "You're not even going to give me a chance?"

Reginalde coughed. Then he tented his fingers and said, "It's nothing personal, Jesse. Thomas has been with us for ten years; Davis has been with us for nearly twelve years. This is a business decision, that's all. The financials don't justify *three* senior management employees to oversee the former Berkshire Hills Property Associates portfolio. The portfolio will be divided up between Thomas and Davis. They're both capable of taking on the additional responsibility. Like I said, it's a business decision. It's all about the numbers."

I was numb, couldn't comprehend that this was happening. "So, what's the next step? I've never been through this before."

"You'll likely be able to collect unemployment for a period of time, until you find a new job. You'll need to remove all of your personal items from your office tonight. I'll stay as long as you need so you can pack up your things."

Fifteen minutes later, all of my personal items were packed in a cardboard box. I dropped my key ring on Reginalde Kalhume's desk on my way out. He was on the phone again. I didn't wait for him to finish his call to say good-bye.

Chapter 5

Mariana was sitting at the kitchen table perusing an Aruba brochure when I got home. Paul was at a friend's house; it was just the two of us.

"Hi honey," she said when I stepped into the kitchen. She stood up to give me a kiss. "What's wrong?" Mariana read me like a book. She immediately sensed that something was out of kilter.

I sighed. "Well, it looks like we might not be going to Aruba in February."

Mariana looked at me with concerned eyes. "No?"

"…I got laid off today."

Mariana pulled me into an embrace. "Oh, *meu amor*."

We stayed locked in each other's arms for a long time. Eventually, I pulled away and looked into her eyes. I was shaking; my voice quivered as I told her about my day. Mariana listened intently as I gave her the play-by-play details of being laid off. She had always been a great listener.

"Stupid people," she said. "Stupid company. It's their loss. You will find a much better job." Mariana always spoke her mind. She was never one to suppress her thoughts.

"Thanks honey." It felt good to unload my burden.

*****

Friday night was *family* night at our home. But this one would be an exception. "I need to play hockey," I told Mariana after a light dinner.

Mariana fully understood. She knew me better than anyone. She gave me a hug and said, "Go."

I changed into sweats and retrieved my hockey bag and stick from the attic. Then I tossed them into the back of the SUV and drove across town to the Beldon Ice Arena. I had no idea if the ice was available or if the rink was even open. I hadn't skated in years.

*****

The rink was deserted when I arrived. The skate shop and concession booth were closed; the stands were empty. But a movement at the far end of the rink caught my eye. An older man. He had apparently seen me, too. He was heading my way.

"Jesse Maclean?" he asked as he neared.

"Hi, Ben."

"Been a long time, son."

"Yes it has."

We shook hands, and Ben put his hand on my shoulder. "Good to see you, son."

"Good to see you too, Ben."

Back in high school, I worked in the skate shop part-time. Ben was my boss. I was surprised he was still working there. The man was getting up there in years.

Ben gave me his thoughts about this season's Beldon High School hockey team. And we talked about the Bruins for a few minutes. Then he looked down at my hockey bag and the stick resting on top of it.

"I was about to run the Zamboni," he said. "But I've got some things to catch up on. The ice is yours for the next forty minutes if you want it."

"Thanks, Ben. I appreciate it."

I headed into the locker room and laced up my skates. I hadn't been in the locker room since the final game of my senior year at Beldon High. I had only skated a few times since high school.

After lacing up my skates, I pulled on my hockey gloves, removed a puck from the hockey bag, and grabbed my stick. Then I headed out onto the ice.

I had always found solace on the ice. When my father was serving his tour in Vietnam during my youth, pond hockey provided a distraction from my constant worries about him. In high school, when I had troubles, I skated them out during hockey practice.

I skated hard. After ten minutes on the ice, I broke a sweat. I pushed myself, skating up and down the rink, stick-handling the puck and taking shots on the empty net.

My legs cramped after a half hour. I was out of shape, but skated on. My shirt was sweat-soaked, and I was sucking wind by the time Ben fired up the Zamboni. My mind was clearing, though. The ice time was just what I needed. I waved to Ben as I left the ice and headed into the locker room.

Chapter 6

Upon being laid off, some people take advantage of the situation and enjoy a period of downtime before searching for a new job. I was not in a position to do so.

I got up at five-thirty Saturday morning, showered, got dressed, and made a pot of coffee. I was at the kitchen table firing up my laptop at six o'clock. It was time to update my resume.

I perused various resume-building websites on the Internet for most of the morning, and then spent a few hours at the Beldon Public Library doing additional research. The afternoon was spent updating my resume. I went through more than a dozen drafts. By five o'clock that evening—eleven hours after I started—I finally had a resume that adequately summed up my employment history and qualifications.

For dinner, Mariana brought home takeout from an Italian restaurant across town—a luxury we could no longer afford. I was famished, having skipped lunch; hadn't had anything to eat all day other than two pieces of toast. I finished dinner in record time.

After dinner, I went back to the kitchen table and fired up the laptop again. Mariana quickly sensed that tonight would not be movie night. She kissed me on the cheek and went upstairs to read.

My evening was spent drafting a cover letter. While not as time consuming as updating my resume, it took much longer than I had expected. It was eleven o'clock by the time I had a cover letter that seemed satisfactory. Mariana was already asleep when I climbed into bed. It was not our usual relaxing Saturday evening.

*****

At six o'clock Sunday morning, I was back at the kitchen table in front of the laptop. With my resume updated and a cover letter drafted, I got down to business and searched for jobs: senior-level property management positions.

It quickly became apparent that property management positions in Massachusetts were few and far between at that time. I checked all of the major job search websites and posted my resume on them. Next, I made a list of every major property management firm I knew of in Massachusetts. Then I searched the Internet for additional property management firms and added more firms to the list. After that, I visited the website for each firm on the list and searched for employment opportunities.

The list wasn't limited to western Massachusetts. I included Springfield, Worcester, and Boston firms, too. By the end of the day, I had come across just four senior-level property management positions that seemed to be a fit for my qualifications. There were other jobs out there in the industry, but they were entry level positions—positions that wouldn't pay enough to cover my monthly debt. I submitted my resume and cover letter online and applied for each of the four positions.

I gave Bill a call afterward. He'd been through this before. Maybe he'd have some suggestions.

"That's tough," he said, when I broke the news. "Sorry, man. You'll bounce back though. Don't worry."

Bill had just been hired by a software company in Worcester. He hadn't been unemployed long. There were a lot more jobs available in his profession, however.

Bill briefed me on the basics of filing for unemployment. He gave me an overview of how the unemployment system worked. "You can expect to receive a check for about half of what you were making previously," he said, "and it's not indefinite. You can only collect unemployment for a limited period of time."

I had never collected unemployment before. Besides Bill, the only people I knew who had collected unemployment were a few cooks.

Bill and I worked on Cape Cod the summer before our senior year of college. We lived in a rooming house. Bill waited tables and I worked on a framing crew. There were a half dozen other guys living in the rooming house, and all of them were a few years older than Bill and me. They worked summers at seasonal restaurants on the Cape, and while most of them spent their winters working at ski resorts, a few opted to collect unemployment in the off season.

Bill gave me the name and number of a headhunter, Holly Tabot. I had not considered the possibility of using a headhunter. "Give her a call tomorrow morning," Bill suggested. "Holly landed two jobs for me in the past. She arranged several job interviews this last time around."

"Thanks, Bill. I'll give her a call."

After the conversation with Bill, I sat down at the kitchen table and compiled a list of my monthly expenses. Our lifestyle was not lavish; we had always been conservative, but our expenses were still up there. Our mortgage was hefty, and I had a daughter in college overseas. Thankfully, Anna had received a significant scholarship, but it didn't cover everything.

I added up our monthly expenses: mortgage payment, utility bills, insurance (life, auto, and home), car loans, credit cards, Anna's tuition, cell phone, food, etc…I suddenly regretted the decision to sell our small ranch-style home two years ago.

We now lived in a spacious four bedroom colonial in the upscale Partridge Ridge development in the northern section of town—and our mortgage was much higher than the previous one. The real estate taxes were much higher too.

Just a few years before, we'd had a significant balance in our savings account, but that was before the purchase of our current home and Anna's enrollment in college. We now had $3,552.09 in our savings account—barely enough to cover one month's expenses.

The good news was that I had already paid the November bills. And I had one more paycheck coming from Central New England Real Estate Group.

Mariana worked part-time. She owned a small business—a hand-crafted jewelry booth at a downtown mill building that had been converted to retail space. Her business had never been too profitable though. After paying the rent, supplies, and labor, there was not much left over. We had always used the small income from her business for discretionary spending.

The reality was that we'd be in dire straits come January unless I found a job quickly. Sleep did not come easy that night. I tossed and turned in bed. It was well past midnight when I finally drifted off.

Chapter 7

Monday, I woke at dawn and continued my job search via the Internet. I researched some additional property management firms, focusing on smaller firms this time. I also researched real estate development companies.

At nine o'clock that morning I called Holly Tabot and introduced myself, mentioned that Bill had referred me. Holly's casual demeanor over the phone threw me off. I had expected someone more aggressive, but it was not an unpleasant surprise.

I told Holly about my employment experience and qualifications. She was up front with me. "Seeking employment at this time of the year can be challenging," she said. "A lot of companies tend to wait until after January 1st to hire new employees, though this is not always the case. The good news is that I have found property management positions for clients in the past. The bad news is there are generally fewer positions open in your industry compared to some other industries. Have you considered doing what you did before?"

I winced. "You mean work as a correspondent?"

"Yes."

"No. I've been away from the business too long now. And the travel is not for me. Those days are behind me."

"Well," Holly replied, "it sounds like you have some great experience and credentials. That's a big plus. But I should warn you that you're probably not going to find a job quite as close to home as the one you had. You may be looking at a lengthier commute."

"I'm planning on that."

"Good. E-mail me your resume, and I'll get the ball rolling."

"I'll do that. Thanks, Holly."

"You got it. I'll be in touch."

The conversation with Holly was sobering. I was aware that it wasn't the ideal time of year to seek employment. I was also aware that a new job would most likely involve a longer commute. Aside from Berkshire Hills Property Associates—now Central New England Real Estate Group—there were no property management firms in the area. There were a number of small real estate brokerage offices, some of which also managed properties—mostly three-deckers and the occasional five or six-unit building—but they were all small scale operations that didn't warrant a fulltime property manager let alone a senior-level property manager.

I e-mailed my resume to Holly. Then my cell phone rang. Caller ID indicated it was Wendy. I answered. "Hey, Wendy."

"They are idiots! I am *so* sorry they let you go. I'm still in shock. They obviously have no idea what they're doing!"

"Thanks, Wendy. You're not in the office right now are you?"

"No. I'm in my car. I'm on my *timed* lunch break. How are you holding up, boss?"

"I'm doing okay." I told her about my job search and mentioned the conversation with Holly.

"Well, when you land a new job—which you surely will—let me know. I want to join you. I'd be out of here right now if I didn't have a daughter to support. I am *not* long for this place."

Wendy and Mariana had a lot in common. Neither of them held their thoughts back. I couldn't help but smile. "You bet, Wendy. Thanks for the call."

"Stay in touch, boss."

"Will do. Hang in there."

*****

I searched the Internet and scoured online job boards for property management positions each day that week. I also continually checked my e-mail for news from Holly and for replies relating to jobs I had applied for. It was the longest week I could recall. Then, on Friday afternoon, Holly called.

"Good news," she announced. "You have an interview next Thursday morning at nine o'clock."

My heart raced. "Excellent!"

Holly informed me that the interview was for a director of property management position with Hampden & Hampshire Property Management, Inc. Their corporate office was in the outskirts of Springfield—a mere forty minute drive from Beldon, far closer than Boston. I was familiar with the firm. They had a solid reputation, and as their name implied, they managed property in Hampden County and Hampshire County. I hadn't come across the position on their website previously and was suddenly grateful to Bill for referring me to Holly.

"I've got to run," Holly said. "But we'll catch up early next week to talk more and discuss strategies for the interview."

"Thanks so much, Holly!"

"You bet. Have a good weekend. *Ciao*."

*****

Mariana was so happy for me when I told her the news that night. She cooked her famous triple-cheese lasagna, and we shared a bottle of white wine over dinner. After dinner, we rented a movie. And for the first time that week, I relaxed. Later that night I enjoyed a deep, peaceful sleep.

Chapter 8

Thursday, November 19

The Hampden & Hampshire Property Management, Inc. corporate office was housed in a renovated brick building. I arrived for the interview twenty minutes early and took a seat on the couch in the reception area. The room was tastefully decorated and very clean.

The receptionist, Cindy, gave me a smile and asked if I would like something to drink: coffee, tea, or water. I politely declined. Cindy answered the phone several times during the time I waited. She was very professional, and I thought that said something about Hampden & Hampshire Property Management, Inc.

During my wait, I reflected on the interview tips Holly had passed along: Take a deep breath if you're nervous; Mention your accomplishments; Stay focused, and look the interviewer in the eye. Holly had also coached me on to how to best respond to certain questions that might be asked. And she provided guidance on questions that I should ask as well.

Hank Jennere, the firm's vice president, stepped into the reception area at nine o'clock. I guessed he was two or three years older than me. The man was well groomed and clad in slacks and a tan oxford shirt with a matching tie. No wingtips for this guy, he wore rubber-soled leather dress shoes, I noticed.

Hank introduced himself, and we shook hands. Then he asked if he could get me anything to drink. I politely declined.

I followed Hank down a hallway and into a spacious conference room that housed an oval walnut table and eight matching ladder-back chairs. Just as we sat down at the table, Hank's cell phone rang. He removed the cell phone from the clip on his belt. "Sorry, Jesse. I'll just be a minute."

Hank answered. "Hey, sport…You bet…I'll be there…No meetings tonight…I promise…See you then."

Hank placed his cell phone on the table. "That was my son. He wanted to know if I was going to be able to make it to his hockey game tonight."

"How old is your son?"

"Twelve."

"What position does he play?"

"Forward."

"Good for him."

"Are you a hockey fan?" Hank asked.

I nodded. "That I am."

Hank grinned. It turned out he was a hockey buff himself and had played hockey in high school, too. We had a lot in common. I liked this guy.

We talked hockey for a good five minutes. Then Hank gave me an overview of the company and told me about some recent acquisitions. He described the company's portfolio and touched on some upcoming capital improvement projects.

Hank reviewed my resume later on and asked some general questions about my experience. Then he said, "Jesse, I'd like to schedule a second interview for the week after next. The owner of the company is out of the office until then. We'll arrange for him to be at the second interview. Our controller, Chad Levinsune, will be there too."

My pulse quickened.

Hank picked up his cell phone and pulled up his calendar. "How does Wednesday, December 2nd at ten o'clock sound?"

"Great," I said. "I look forward to it, Hank."

"Same here, Jesse. It was real good meeting you. Have a great Thanksgiving."

"You, too, Hank. Thanks very much for your time today. The position is exactly what I'm looking for. "

*****

Mariana wrapped her arms around me when I told her about the interview. "You'll get the job! That company is going to be lucky to have you."

"Thanks, *meu amor*."

At dinner that night, Mariana said, "You've been at this job search nonstop; you've put your time in. That company is obviously very interested in you. You should take some time off between now and the next interview. Enjoy a little downtime while you can."

I nodded in agreement. Mariana was absolutely right. Things were looking up. A little downtime would be a gift. Short of a few family vacations, I had worked continuously since graduating from college. The prospect of a little downtime was suddenly very exciting.

After dinner, I went out to the garage. When we had first looked at the house with the realtor, I thought the garage was the perfect place for a workshop. I had intended to set up a workshop in the garage after we moved in and got settled. But times were busy. Two years had passed since the closing, and my tools were still packed in boxes.

I'd always enjoyed woodworking and carpentry. I had a workshop in the basement of my childhood home, and my summers during high school and college were spent working on framing crews and construction sites.

Memories of summers from my youth came flooding back to me as I opened the boxes of tools that had been stored in the garage for the last two years. Inside one box was the Stanley tape measure my first boss had given me. In another box was the well- worn toolbelt I'd bought back in high school. And of course there were the hand tools: crosscut saws, chisels, wrenches, nail sets, a combination square, levels, files, and a vintage block plane that had belonged to my grandfather.

I sketched a plan for a tool bench that night and made a list of the lumber and materials I'd need. I was looking forward to this.

Chapter 9

Thanksgiving

Mariana and I hosted Thanksgiving at our house. There were five guests including Paul, my parents, and my grandparents. My parents had picked up my grandparents at their farm in Vermont the day before. My octogenarian grandparents are quite active for their age.

My grandfather, a World War II veteran, is not one to talk about his wartime experience. Even my father knows very little of his service in Europe. Dad told me that when my grandfather came home from the war, he placed his uniform and accoutrements in a trunk and went to work the following day.

We purchased the turkey at Jenkins Farm along with several side dishes and three pies: apple, pumpkin, and pecan. I attempted to help out in the kitchen, but Mariana, Mom, and my grandmother had things under control; there wasn't much space for a fourth person—and there was a football game on. So I joined Paul, Dad, and my grandfather in the den. Four generations of Maclean men in one room.

Our Thanksgiving dinner was a succulent affair. Nobody cooks turkey like Mariana. Aside from turkey and stuffing, there were mashed potatoes, roast potatoes, a garden salad, sweet potatoes, cornbread, cranberry sauce, and crescent rolls.

It was good catching up with the family. Mom and Dad updated us on their recent trip to Montreal. My grandparents mentioned some happenings on the farm. Mariana talked about her business. And Paul updated everyone on his swim team's stats. I didn't bring up my employment situation. I'd break the news when the new job was in hand.

We ate dessert in the living room by the fireplace, and the conversation shifted to Christmas. My grandfather cleared his throat and said, "If it's okay with everyone, we'd like to host Christmas at our place this year."

"That's right," my grandmother confirmed. "We don't know how much longer we'll be there. You know we've looked at that retirement village across town."

Everyone nodded in agreement. The Maclean clan would celebrate Christmas in Vermont. It was decided that Mom and Dad, both of whom were retired, would head up to Vermont the week before Christmas and stay at my grandparents' farm to help with the holiday preparations. It was hard to believe Christmas was just a month away.

Chapter 10

Wednesday, December 2

I arrived at the Hampden & Hampshire Property Management, Inc. corporate office fifteen minutes early for the second interview. Once again, Cindy offered me something to drink and I politely declined. Hank Jennere stepped into the room at ten o'clock. He greeted me and we shook hands.

"Good to see you, Jesse. How was your Thanksgiving?"

"Great, thanks," I replied. "How about yours?"

Hank smiled. "Superb."

Hank brought me down the hall to the conference room. He introduced me to Brock Jetner, the firm's owner. Then he introduced me to the controller, Chad Levinsune. Both men stood up, and I shook hands with them. They appeared to be in their fifties. Each of them had a copy of my resume in front of them.

"Have a seat," Brock instructed. He motioned to a chair across the table from him.

I made my way over to the chair and sat down. Then the three of them sat down. "Hank tells me good things about you, Jesse," Brock said, taking the lead. "Your resume is impressive. You're one of *three* candidates we've called back for a second interview."

I was surprised to learn that I wasn't the *only* candidate but tried to take the news in stride. I was qualified for the position, after all. And I thought the first interview had gone very well.

Brock Jetner and Chad Levinsune took turns asking me questions. Brock struck me as a humble man; he spoke with enthusiasm. Chad was more reserved. His demeanor was more formal, his questions direct.

Hank interjected with positive feedback as the opportunity arose. It was clear that Hank was pulling for me. I was grateful to him.

The interview lasted a half hour. In closing, Brock smiled and said, "Thanks for coming in, Jesse. We appreciate your time and enjoyed meeting you. We'll be in touch by the end of the week."

I shook hands with Brock and Chad and thanked them for their time and consideration, told them the position was exactly what I was looking for. Then Hank walked me down the hall to the front vestibule.

"I think that went well, Jesse," he said. "As Brock mentioned, we'll be in touch by the end of the week."

"Thanks so much, Hank. I'd welcome the opportunity to work for you."

"Thank you, Jesse. Talk to you soon."

*****

How I wanted that job. How I *needed* that job. I reflected on the interview during the drive home, analyzed my responses to the questions that had been asked, and mulled over the questions that I had asked. There was nothing I could have done better. I thought the interview had gone very well. And how grateful I was to Hank for pulling for me. That was a real plus.

I called Holly on the way home and told her I thought the interview had gone very well. "That's wonderful news," she said, "especially since I haven't come across any other property management job openings. Keep me updated. I'll let you know if I hear anything as well."

"You bet. Thanks again, Holly."

"Sure thing."

When I got home, I immediately e-mailed thank you notes to Hank, Brock, and Chad. I reiterated that the director of property management position was exactly what I was looking for. Then I waited to hear back.

*****

The home phone rang at two o'clock on Friday afternoon.

I picked up the receiver. "Hello."

"Jesse, this is Hank Jennere." My heart raced when I heard Hank's voice.

"Hank, how are you?"

"Jesse…I regret to say that I'm not calling with the news you were hoping for. The position has been filled."

I couldn't believe it. The director of property management position had seemed like a sure thing, a done deal. I was stunned.

"It was a very competitive interview process," Hank explained. "In the end, it was down to you and one other candidate. You were certainly qualified for the position, more than qualified. There was no doubt that you would have excelled in the position…but the other candidate had a few more years of experience, and in all honesty, the other candidate is related to Chad Levinsune—she's Chad's cousin. I'm very sorry to break the news, Jesse. You'll be receiving a letter from us, but I wanted to give you the courtesy of a phone call. I wish you the best of luck, and please don't hesitate to call me if I can ever be of assistance in your job search."

Back to square one. As hard as it was, I thanked Hank for his call. Then I sat down at the kitchen table. I suddenly felt drained. Deflated.

Mariana was at work, and Paul had a swim meet. It was just me at home. The house had never seemed quieter. I must have sat at the kitchen table for an hour lost in thought. Then I got up, grabbed my hockey gear, and headed to the rink.

Chapter 11

I was back at the kitchen table with my laptop at six o'clock Saturday morning. I e-mailed Holly and let her know the outcome of the second interview with Hampden & Hampshire Property Management, Inc. Then I scoured the Internet for property management positions. Again.

Holly was right about the scarcity of employment opportunities at that time of year. I searched all of the usual online job boards, but there were no senior-level property management positions available, just a few entry-level positions.

Reality set in when I paid the monthly bills later that morning. Then it occurred to me that I hadn't filed for unemployment yet. I had been banking on the position at Hampden & Hampshire Property Management, Inc., and I hadn't thought it would be necessary to file for unemployment. Bill's words came back to me: "You can expect to receive a check for about half of what you were making previously."

Nobody in our family had ever filed for unemployment before that I knew of; I wasn't looking forward to being the first, but knew it was inevitable. I planned to file on Monday.

That afternoon I went out to the garage and spent some time in my newly-constructed workshop. I took in the tool bench and looked over the hand tools neatly arranged on the shelving and hooks.

How therapeutic it had been to work with my hands again. Using the circular saw and table saw to cut lumber for the tool bench had brought back memories of summers spent working construction. I'd always enjoyed carpentry and had become lost in my work as I constructed the tool bench in the days before Thanksgiving.

As I reflected back on the excitement of constructing the tool bench and how good it felt to work with my hands again, I suddenly wondered if there were any construction jobs available in town. A job that might pay more than an unemployment check—a job to get me by until I came across a property management position. Why hadn't I thought of this before?

I hopped into the SUV a few minutes later and headed off to search for construction sites I could visit Monday morning to inquire about work.

Though it was only early December, Beldon was already imbued with holiday spirit. An evergreen garland stretched across the top of Main Street, and the downtown storefronts were festooned in holiday décor. As in previous years, Fiske's Department Store, the largest of the town's retailers, was the most vibrantly decorated business on Main Street. A pine wreath with a bright crimson bow and silver bells hung on the establishment's entry door.

Beldon's annual holiday parade was in full swing as I reached the business district. Throngs of people were gathered on the downtown sidewalks and Main Street was congested with traffic—a rare occurrence. I thought back to the days when Mariana and I brought the kids to the holiday parade. We never missed it when the kids were younger.

For the most part, Beldon was still the quintessential small New England town of my youth, though it had not been spared from development. The Woolworth's, the movie theater, and the A&P were gone now. And Coolidge Junior High was now Coolidge Condominium.

I bypassed Main Street and headed toward the western edge of town, where I knew of two housing developments under construction. One was a single family subdivision, the other a townhouse development. A sign was posted at each site with the name of the builder.

I stopped by both construction sites and wrote down the phone numbers listed under the builders' names. Then I drove to the southern section of town where there was an office building under construction. I noted the builder's phone number there, too. I had three prospects to visit on Monday morning.

Chapter 12

December 7

After a quick breakfast on Monday morning, I headed to the southern section of town and stopped by the office building construction site. My visit was a short one. The foreman informed me there were no job openings. He recommended I try again after the first of the year.

After that I made my way to the western part of town and stopped by the townhouse development. The general contractor seemed to have some interest when I told him I had framing experience. But he quickly wrote me off when I disclosed that I had been removed from the business for a while and hadn't actually framed houses for a number of years.

My expectations were not high when I pulled into the third job site, the residential subdivision. The name of the builder—Jaimes O'Malluy Company—was etched on a sign tacked to a newly-constructed split level home.

A pickup truck stopped along the curb of a cul-de-sac just before I arrived, and I parked behind it. A man stepped out carrying a cardboard tray containing four cups of coffee. He set the tray down on a stack of plywood when I caught up with him. I correctly guessed he was the builder.

Jaimes O'Malluy was an Irishman. I pegged him to be in his late fifties or early sixties. One look at him told me he was *old school*. The man wore a canvas nail apron rather than a leather toolbelt, and tucked in his back pocket was a wooden folding tape measure.

Jaimes O'Malluy listened as I told him about my experience in the trade. He asked about my familiarity with power tools—table saws, circular saws, belt sanders, miter boxes, and nail guns. I told him I had used all of the tools before, and more, which was the truth. I also told him I had spent a summer as a "cutter" on a framing crew. His eyebrows lifted when I mentioned that.

"One of my guys—Ralph—just quit last week," Jaimes O'Malluy informed me. "Ralph decided on a career change. He found work on a scalloping boat in New Bedford. "How soon can you start?"

A surge of adrenaline shot through me. "Is tomorrow too soon?"

"Be here at seven-thirty."

I inquired about the pay and was pleasantly surprised. It turned out that I'd make slightly more working for the Jaimes O'Malluy Company than I would by collecting unemployment—if I was up to the work. It still wasn't enough to cover my monthly expenses, but I was better off than when I woke up that morning.

"See you at seven-thirty tomorrow morning," Jaimes O'Malluy said. "Oh, next week will be a short one. We're just working through Wednesday, the 16th. Then we're off for seven days. I'm heading south for the holidays. We'll start up again the Monday after Christmas."

"That works for me. See you tomorrow morning."

Chapter 13

Not counting Jaimes O'Malluy, I was the oldest person on the crew. The other guys—Mauricio, Taylor, and Scott—were in their twenties. All of them were in far better shape than me.

Most of the general contractors I worked for previously had subbed out a lot of work: framing, roofing, drywall, insulation, finish carpentry, etc. It was common practice in the industry. But I quickly learned it wasn't Jaimes O'Malluy's practice.

On Tuesday, my first day on the job, we finished roofing one unit in the morning, and in the afternoon we sheathed the adjacent unit and installed windows. It rained on Wednesday and we spent the day indoors insulating walls and installing flooring. Thursday was sunny and brisk. Our day was spent framing.

Each day, one of the members of the crew brought coffee. On Friday it was my turn. I stopped by Eugenia's Bakery on the way to the job site that morning. Back in my youth, Eugenia had given my friends and me day-old muffins free of charge. I was waiting in line reflecting on those days when someone tapped me on the shoulder. I turned around. It was Bud Clements, a plumbing contractor.

"Hey, Jesse," he said. "I wasn't sure it was you at first."

My attire, along with the tape measure and hammer holster on my belt surely must have taken him by surprise.

"Bud, how are you?"

He frowned. "I've been better."

"I know the feeling," I said.

"I was sure sorry to hear about your situation, Jesse. Truly sorry. It was very unprofessional of Central New England Real Estate Group, if you ask me."

"Thanks, Bud."

"Things didn't work out for me when they took over either," Bud said. "They brought in some plumbing outfit from Boston."

"Sorry to hear that, Bud." I knew this must have hit him hard financially. Bud had done a lot of business with Berkshire Hill Property Associates. If a building needed a new boiler or hot water heater, Bud took care of it. His work was top notch, and he was very responsive. His rates were quite reasonable, too.

"Yeah, well, I have other work lined up," Bud stated. "I'll tell you one thing though. The former Berkshire Hill Property Associates clients are *not* happy with this new outfit."

"No?"

"Not at all. You know that architect, Steve Hartnick, who owns the office building across town?"

"I do."

"Well, a pipe burst in his building a few weeks back. Happened on a Friday night. Steve called Central New England Real Estate Group repeatedly that weekend. Their maintenance crew never responded. When Steve's first floor tenants arrived for work on Monday morning, the carpet was under a foot of water. There was an awful lot of damage. Steve is an easy going guy, but I heard he was ticked."

"I can imagine."

"The owner of Beldon Gardens isn't too pleased with the new management company either," Bud went on. "Beldon Gardens had no heat or hot water for two days last week."

"*Two days?*"

Bud nodded. "I kid you not."

Just then, it was my turn at the counter. I ordered five large coffees from Eugenia's daughter, Ana Flavia.

"Good seeing you," I told Bud on my way out.

"Same here, Jesse. You take care now."

*****

My cell phone rang during lunch. Caller ID indicated it was Wendy. I picked it up. "Hey there, Wendy. How goes it?"

"How are you doing, boss?"

It was good to hear her voice. "I'm doing all right. How are *you* doing?"

"Ugh. This place is not the same. It's a whole different ball game. I don't see myself here for long."

"Sorry, Wendy."

"Thanks, boss. By the way, Steve Hartnick called this morning. He asked about you, wanted to know where you're working now. He's not happy with Central New England Real Estate Group."

"So I hear. I bumped into Bud Clements this morning. He told me about the problem at Steve's building. What a shame."

Wendy sighed. "It is. I have the feeling Steve won't be renewing his management contract."

"He doesn't have much time to think about it," I said. "His management contract expires at the end of the month. The same as the management contracts for the other two investor-owned properties."

"I know. We mailed a new contract to Steve and the other investors several weeks ago. They have yet to sign them."

"Times change."

"Yes, unfortunately, they do. Oh, Giuseppe Moretti left a few messages for you. I don't think he knows that you're not here anymore."

"Thanks, Wendy. I'll plan to give him a call."

"Okay, boss. Listen, my *timed* lunch break is over. Time for me to return to my desk. It was *good* hearing your voice again. Have a good weekend."

"You, too, Wendy. Stay in touch."

"You can count on it."

I felt bad for Wendy, wished there was something I could do for her. She deserved better.

Chapter 14

A cold front pushed down from the north the following week. I wore long johns under my work clothes. I bought a wool hat and a pair of insulated gloves at Fiske's Department Store. Last week I had blisters on my hands; this week I had calluses. I was toughening up.

Mauricio and Taylor hummed Christmas carols as we worked. Scott was the quietest of the three, but he was in a festive mood, too—Scott tacked a wreath on the gable end of the house we were framing.

Had it been any other year, I would have been caught up in the season, too. I wasn't exactly in a festive mood. My financial situation was continually at the forefront of my thoughts. Even though I was working now, my financial status was growing more precarious with each passing day.

*****

Though I kept in touch with Holly via e-mail and continued to search the Internet for property management positions each evening, I had pretty much written off the possibility of finding a real estate management position for the time being. I needed to accept the fact that I'd be swinging a hammer for the foreseeable future.

A lot of thoughts ran through my head during the course of each work day. I wondered what the New Year would bring. Would we need to sell the SUV? Or the house? There was Anna's education too. I was consumed by financial worries.

At the end of the day on Wednesday, Jaimes O'Malluy gave each of us a hundred dollar Christmas bonus. I thought it was quite generous of the man, especially in my case. I had been employed by him for less than two weeks. "Have a great Christmas," he said. "See you lads on the 28th."

Chapter 15

My mother called after dinner that evening. "Your father and I have the flu," she said. "It looks like we're not going to be able to make it up to Vermont this week to help your grandparents prepare for Christmas…Do you think there's any way you might be able to take some time off work and head up there to help out?" I still hadn't told my parents about my employment situation.

"Actually…yes," I answered. Why not? It had been quite a while since I'd been to my grandparents' farm. And I had the time.

"That's wonderful, honey. Thanks so much. I know it will mean a lot to Grandma and Grandpa."

"No problem, Mom. I'll give them a call. You and Dad rest up and feel better."

"Thanks, sweetheart. Everything well on your end?"

"Yes. All is well here, Mom."

"Okay. Love you. Hugs and kisses for Mariana and Paul and give Anna our best when you speak with her. Bye."

I caught up with Mariana in the living room. She was unpacking a box of Christmas decorations. I saw she had placed the old Christmas Tin on the bay windowsill. I admired the tin for a few moments, recalling the holiday mementos and gifts we had placed inside it over the years.

"Hey," Mariana said, breaking my reverie.

"Hi, honey."

I told Mariana the news and she said, "Great. Go for it. You've always enjoyed visiting your grandparents."

It was true. I did enjoy spending time with my grandparents. My grandparents' farm was located in central Vermont. They bought the farm the year after my grandfather returned from overseas, and they'd lived there ever since.

"I'll give them a call," I said. "I'll plan to head up there tomorrow."

Mariana wrapped her arms around me. "I'd join you, but duty calls. It's going to be a busy week for the business."

"I know. Maybe Paul can join me."

Mariana shook her head. "School doesn't let out for Christmas break until next week, and he has swim practice."

"That's right. Well, it will be different without you guys there," I said.

Mariana smiled. "We'll all be there for Christmas."

"That we will."

Chapter 16

I filled a travel mug with coffee on Thursday morning and tossed my duffel bag in the SUV. I had packed enough clothes for five days—I wasn't planning to stay that long, but wanted to be prepared should my stay be extended due to inclement weather.

As I was about to pull out of the driveway it occurred to me that it might be prudent to bring some tools. My grandparents' place was likely in need of repairs. I went to the workshop, grabbed my toolbox, and tossed it in the back of the SUV.

On the way out of town, I cut across Main Street and passed by North Church. A colossal evergreen wreath was suspended over the church's double-door entrance.

A few minutes later, I passed by Johnson Pond. A half dozen kids were playing pond hockey. I couldn't help but smile. How my friends and I loved to play pond hockey when we were their age. We spent countless hours on the pond ice back then. Pond hockey season was the best time of the year for us. We lived for it.

When I reached the western edge of town, I turned onto Route 7 and headed north. It hadn't snowed yet, but the mountains were still picturesque. The evergreens contrasted sharply with the barren hardwoods.

I tuned the radio to a station playing Christmas carols and continued north on Route 7. I eventually crossed the state line and drove through the towns of Pownal, Manchester, and Rutland, before turning northeast onto Route 4. Soon, patches of snow could be seen through breaks in the trees along the side of the road. By the time I turned onto Route 100, the ground was blanketed with six inches of fresh snow. The skiers would be happy.

I stayed on Route 100 for some time, passing through Pittsfield, Stockbridge, and Rochester. Then I turned east onto Kotch Brook Road.

Kotch Brook paralleled the road. I recalled the times I took Paul and Anna fishing there when they were toddlers. Both of them caught their first trout in the small brook.

The covered bridge up ahead brought back more memories. I had been fascinated by the bridge as a child; we didn't have covered bridges in our area. I admired the post and beam construction as I drove over the bridge.

Kotch Brook Road cut north just beyond the bridge. I followed it for five minutes and drove by dairy farms, fields, and woodland. Then the general store loomed in the distance. As a child, no trip to my grandparents' farm was complete unless we stopped at the general store for penny candy and an ice cream from the vintage soda fountain in the back of the store.

Shortly after passing by the general store, I turned off Kotch Brook Road and headed up the snow-crusted lane to my grandparents' farm. The lane rose in elevation as it weaved through a stand of evergreens.

The scene at the end of the lane was something out of a Norman Rockwell painting: a white farmhouse and a red barn flanked by snow-covered fields and orchards, all of it set against the majestic Green Mountains.

It was just past noon when I pulled up to the farmhouse. Smoke emanated from the farmhouse's chimney. I parked the SUV next to my grandfather's old Ford pickup.

My grandparents—Iris and Gerald Maclean—stepped out onto the farmers porch as I was removing my duffel bag from the SUV. They were all smiles as was their golden retriever, Penny. "Welcome, sweetheart!" my grandmother called.

"Thanks, Grandma. Great to be up here again."

Penny bolted from the porch and charged across the yard, yelping. She reached me in seconds. I bent down and scratched her ears. "Hello, girl. It's good to see you, too."

My grandmother embraced me in a hug when I reached the porch. My grandfather watched us with an amused smile. He was clad in his usual outfit—dark green cotton work pants and a matching shirt under a green and black checkered wool coat.

"Hey there, Jesse," he said. "Thanks for coming up to God's country." We shook hands. His grip was as strong as ever.

"Glad to be here," I said. "I've been looking forward to it."

My grandmother shivered. "Let's go inside," she said. "You're just in time for lunch."

"Sounds great, Grandma. I've been thinking about your cooking since Massachusetts."

*****

I put my duffel bag in the bedroom where I'd stayed in during childhood visits. Then I headed downstairs to the kitchen to join my grandparents for lunch.

My grandparents' kitchen had fascinated me as a child. The vintage pressed tin ceiling, hand-hewn beams, and wide pine floors were from another time. So, too, was the cast iron hand pump beside the white porcelain sink.

My grandfather saw me looking at the hand pump. "It doesn't work anymore," he stated. "Disconnected the water feed when we put the new sink in. Couldn't bring myself to remove that old hand pump."

"Glad you didn't," I said. "The kitchen wouldn't be the same without it."

Lunch consisted of homemade tomato soup and grilled cheese sandwiches with bacon on thick sourdough bread. As we ate, my grandparents inquired about Mariana and the kids. They mentioned how glad they were that the family was coming up for Christmas.

My grandparents also talked about some happenings around town—a church supper, a holiday bazaar, the Christmas pageant at the elementary school, a food drive. There was mention of a neighboring farm that offered horse-drawn sleigh rides.

After lunch, I donned my jacket, hat, and boots. It was thirty-two degrees and sunny outside. Perfect weather for our mission.

My grandfather and I stepped out of the house and headed toward his old Ford pickup. On the way across the yard, he grabbed an axe from the woodpile.

Penny accompanied us. I lowered the pickup's tailgate, and she eagerly hopped in back. My grandfather placed the axe in the bed of the truck and handed me the keys. "You drive."

"Gladly."

We climbed into the cab, and the engine turned over on the third try. After letting the truck warm up for a few minutes, I drove around back and headed up the farm road that cut between the hay field and the apple orchard.

Deer tracks crisscrossed the orchard, and there were areas of exposed earth at the base of apple trees where deer had foraged for apples. I flashed back to a moonlit summer night in my youth where my grandfather and I had sat on a flat rock at the southern edge of the orchard. We watched a half dozen deer feed on fallen apples that evening. One of the deer was a mature buck. Moonlight glistened on the buck's antlers.

The farm road ended at the base of the mountain. I parked the truck, and as we disembarked, Penny leaped out of the truck's bed and made her way into the undergrowth. A partridge exploded from the cover. Penny yelped and bolted up the mountain in pursuit.

"Fool dog," my grandfather smiled. "She still has some puppy in her."

"That she does." Like my grandparents, Penny had aged gracefully over the years.

My grandfather grabbed the axe from the truck bed, and we followed a deer trail through the undergrowth and slowly made our way up the mountain to the tree lot—a stand of Douglas fir.

More childhood memories came flooding back to me…riding in the wagon behind the tractor on the way to the mountain…planting saplings on the mountainside…tapping trees for maple syrup…picking apples in the orchard.

Once we reached the tree lot, it didn't take us long to select a tree. We decided on a thick six-footer along the northern edge of the tree lot. "It's a fine one," my grandfather remarked as he raked his hand through the vibrant bluish-green needles on one of the tree's lower branches. Penny barked in agreement.

The axe blade had been freshly sharpened; felling the tree was quick work.

As I dragged the tree down the mountain afterward with Penny at my heels, I recalled helping my grandfather haul Christmas trees down the mountain back in my youth when he supplied his friends and neighbors with Christmas trees.

*****

When we pulled up to the farmhouse, I noted a large pile of split firewood in the front yard. "Looks like we just missed Earl," my grandfather said.

"Earl?"

"The guy I buy my firewood from," my grandfather clarified.

"Looks to be about a cord?" I guessed.

"Yep. You're right on the money. Should last us a while."

"I'll stack it this afternoon," I said.

My grandfather grinned. "I'll take you up on that."

When we stepped into the farmhouse, my grandmother was in the kitchen removing a loaf of hot pumpkin bread from the oven. The air was pungent with the aroma of pumpkin, nutmeg, and cinnamon. Each holiday season my grandmother baked pumpkin bread for friends and relatives. She had been doing so for as long as I could remember.

"Will there be some pumpkin bread left for desert tonight?" I inquired.

My grandmother flashed a smile. "Yes, but you don't need to wait till then." She cut a slice for me and set it on a plate. "Here you go," she said as she handed the plate to me.

"Thanks, Grandma. Where would you like the tree?"

"The usual place—in the living room, to the left of the fireplace."

"You got it."

"The tree stand is in the attic," she said.

"I'll get it."

"Thanks. There's a box of Christmas decorations beside the tree stand. If you could bring the box down, too, that would be swell."

"I'm on it."

"I'll stoke the fire," my grandfather volunteered.

I went up to the attic, retrieved the tree stand and the box of Christmas decorations, and carried them downstairs to the living room. Then I placed the box of decorations on the floor by the couch and set the tree stand up in the corner to the left of the fireplace. After that, I went out to the truck to get the tree.

My grandfather and I placed the Douglas fir in the tree stand and wrestled it into place—it was a two-person job. My grandmother stepped into the living room a few moments later and handed me a pitcher of water. "We'll let the branches fall into place today," she said. "We can decorate it tomorrow."

"Sounds like a plan," I said, emptying the pitcher of water into the stand.

I spent the rest of the afternoon stacking firewood on the farmers porch at the front of the house. The manual labor felt good.

As I hauled firewood to the porch, I noted a half dozen floor boards in need of replacement. A project for the following day. Nightfall was edging in. A coyote howled in the distance as I finished stacking the last of the firewood.

*****

Dinner consisted of beef stew, homemade bread, and a garden salad. We ate at the kitchen table.

For dessert, my grandmother served warm pumpkin bread topped with a dollop of vanilla ice cream. After dessert, she made a pot of tea and the three of us retreated to the living room.

I got a fire going in the fireplace, and my grandfather and I watched a college hockey game on television while my grandmother worked on her latest quilt. Penny was curled on the braided rug in front of the fireplace. It was good to be there.

I don't know whether it was attributable to the country air, the hearty meal, or the manual labor, but I slept very soundly that night.

Chapter 17

The following morning, after a quick shower, I reached into my duffel bag for some clean clothes. My hand brushed something solid in the bag as I removed a flannel shirt. This took me by surprise. I had only packed clothing in the duffel bag, nothing else.

Curious, I peered into the bag—and saw the Christmas Tin. Mariana must have packed it. Why, I didn't know. Perhaps it was intended as our contribution toward holiday décor. I'd have to ask Mariana about it when I got home.

After getting dressed, I picked up the Christmas Tin and carried it downstairs to the living room. I placed it on the mantel above the fireplace and headed into the kitchen. My grandmother was sipping coffee at the kitchen table. On the stovetop were two pans. One pan contained scrambled eggs. The other contained my grandmother's famous home fries.

She stood up when I entered the room and gave me a kiss on the cheek. "Sleep well, sweetheart?"

"I did."

"Glad to hear it. Ready for some breakfast?"

"Very ready."

My grandmother grabbed a plate from the cupboard as I took a seat at the kitchen table. She spooned heaping portions of scrambled eggs and home fries onto the plate and placed it before me on the table.

"Thanks, Grandma. Where's Grandpa?"

"You just missed him. He left for the VFW Hall a few minutes ago. There's a pancake breakfast there this morning. His friend, Bronson, stopped by to pick him up."

"Is Bronson a World War II veteran, too?"

My grandmother shook her head. "No. Bronson is a little younger than your grandfather. Bronson served in Korea. They were going to wake you to see if you wanted to join them, but I told them to let you sleep."

*****

After breakfast, I grabbed my toolbox from the SUV and brought it over to the front porch. Then I went out to my grandfather's workshop in the barn to search for floorboards. The workshop had been a place of wonder to me as a kid. I'd spent hours there in my youth, helping my grandfather with various projects.

My grandfather kept assorted nails and screws in small glass jars neatly lined up along the back edge of his workbench. Resting on the workbench were hand tools: hammers, crosscut saws, a jig saw, an old hand drill, a block plane, and a wooden folding tape measure. On the floor on each side of the workbench were stacks of boards.

I removed the rotted floorboards from the porch that morning. Then I cut new floorboards with my grandfather's vintage table saw. I was in my element and was soon lost in my work. The next thing I knew, my grandmother stepped out onto the porch and announced that the midday meal was ready. I removed my toolbelt and headed inside for lunch—hot chili and cornbread.

*****

My grandmother was in the living room unpacking Christmas decorations as I finished my lunch.

"Jesse," she called, "would you mind getting a fire going in the fireplace after lunch?"

"Sure thing. Be right there."

"Take your time, and enjoy your lunch. No rush. There's more chili and cornbread if you're still hungry.

"Thanks, Grandma. I couldn't eat another bite."

When I stepped into the living room a few minutes later, my grandmother was standing in front of the fireplace. She was looking at the Christmas Tin on the mantel.

"It's a Christmas Tin," I informed her.

"So I see. Christmas Tins were quite popular years back… This is *something.*"

"Mariana packed it in my duffel bag."

"I'm glad she did. The tin appears to have been handcrafted?"

"Yes," I confirmed. "It dates back to the Depression."

My grandmother's eyebrows lifted. "I don't recall seeing it before. Is it from Mariana's side of the family?"

"No. The Christmas Tin was bequeathed to me by an elderly customer on my paper route back in my youth."

I could tell my grandmother was intrigued by the Christmas Tin, and I told her the history of the tin as I helped her unpack the decorations from the box I had brought down from the attic. I also told her about the

75

gifts and mementos my family had placed in the tin over the years. I mentioned some of the stories behind the older mementos in the Christmas Tin as well.

"What a lovely tradition," she remarked.

The Christmas decorations in the box from the attic spanned decades. I recognized some red ball-shaped ornaments that had been popular when I was a kid. And there were older glass ornaments which I guessed were from the 1950s. There was a string of lights—the multi-colored incandescent-type that had been popular before LED Christmas lights became the norm. There was even some old lead tinsel in the box.

We had unpacked about half of the decorations in the box when my grandmother headed to the kitchen for coffee. While she was gone, I placed a few more logs in the fireplace. Then I strung the lights on the tree, starting at the top, as was my custom.

My grandmother returned with our coffees, and we continued to take our time unpacking ornaments and decorations. We hung ornaments on the tree as we went along, slowly sipping coffee in the process.

Most of the decorations and ornaments had been removed from the cardboard box when I noticed a small wooden box at the bottom. The small box had a hinged lid that was secured with ornate brass hinges. The box was about the size of a brick.

My grandmother gently removed the small wooden box and placed it on the coffee table. I watched as she slowly opened the lid.

Inside the box were two objects. Both were wrapped in white tissue paper. My grandmother's eyes sparkled. Intuition told me that the objects underneath the tissue paper were special, likely sentimental.

"Would you like to hear a Christmas story?" my grandmother asked.

"Absolutely. I'm always up for a Christmas story."

"Do you have some time?"

I smiled. "Time is something I have plenty of right now."

My grandmother took a sip of her coffee. She set her mug down on the coffee table and stared into the embers in the fireplace. Then she drifted back over the years...

Chapter 18

December 15, 1933

Iris Jansen peered into the coffee bean canister and sighed. The canister was almost empty. Coffee beans were a lifeline now—coffee was the family's only source of income aside from the remaining barrel of apples from the fall harvest.

Iris scooped coffee beans into a cup. She reflected back on the past year as she poured the coffee beans into the grinder and worked the hand crank to grind the beans.

Iris's family had fared better than most in the area during the hard times—until her father's accident. Her father, Wilfred Jansen, hauled logs down at the sawmill that autumn. He and a co-worker had been loading logs onto a wagon with skid poles when Wilfred's skid pole broke. He was toppled by a log, and within seconds his left arm, leg, and collar bone were broken.

With Iris's father laid up and out of work, the family was in dire straits. Then things turned even worse. Two weeks after the accident, the bank padlocked its doors. The family's meager savings were gone. Just like that.

That summer, Iris had helped her mother clean summer homes up at the lake. But by that time, the once bustling summer cottage colony that had formerly been occupied by well-to-do folks from the big cities—New York, Boston, and Philadelphia—was all but deserted.

The family's only means of income now was their small roadside farm stand beside the house. A handwritten sign tacked to the front of the stand advertised the only products the family now had for sale: hot coffee and cider.

Before the Depression, the Jansen's sold vegetables, jams, pastries, muffins, homemade pies, and refreshments at the farm stand. The stand was conveniently located on the road to the lake, the same road that people traveled to and from Canada. But the tourist industry was practically nonexistent. There were very few cars on the road now.

Most people could no longer afford to drive. If someone couldn't afford to pay seven cents for a loaf of bread, they certainly couldn't afford to pay thirty cents for a gallon of gas. Besides, most people who had owned cars had already sold them—for what little money they could get.

To make ends meet, people sold practically everything they owned—hand tools, clothing, dishware, pots, pans, furniture. You name it. Iris's mother sold her sewing machine, an electric fan, an iron, and other household items.

Some people even sold their beds for food money. That was the case with Mrs. Carhardt, a widow who had five hungry children to feed. She and her children slept on pallets now. The elderly couple down the street, the Gilberts, wasn't any better off. The same with the steeplejack, Mr. Burns, who lived in a shack next door. He had been out of work for more than a year.

Iris brewed a pot of coffee. The enamel on the coffee pot was worn out and chipped in numerous places—a sign of the times. When the coffee was ready, Iris carried the pot out to the farm stand. Her younger sister, Sarah, was inside the stand tending the woodstove, and their mother was back at the house caring for the baby who had croup. Their father was home, as well. He was bedridden and would be for some time to come.

"Any customers?" Iris asked as she stepped inside the stand and placed the coffee pot on top of the woodstove.

Sarah shook her head. "None. Just like yesterday and the day before."

"Maybe a new sign would help," Iris said in a hopeful tone.

"Maybe."

The sisters remained at the stand all day. A half dozen cars drove by during that time. But none of them stopped.

When they got home that night there was a man at the front door seeking work—chores that could be performed in exchange for food. Their mother shook her head no. "I wish we *could* give you some work," she told the man. He tipped his tattered hat and walked away.

Dinner that evening consisted of thin vegetable soup. Again. The vegetables in the root cellar were vital to their survival at this point. There were no soup kitchens in their part of northern Vermont. Unlike in the city, there were no handouts to be had. The family was on its own just like the all of the other townfolk.

Iris brought a bowl of soup upstairs to her father. His forehead was beaded with sweat. He winced in pain as he propped himself up in bed to sip the soup.

"How are you, Papa?"

"Getting better every day," he lied. "I'll be up and about before you know it."

After supper, Iris and Sarah read in front of the woodstove. Firelight was the only source of illumination in the room. Like many families, the Jansen's could no longer afford to pay for electricity. They used the kerosene lamps sparingly. There was no telling if they would be able to afford to buy kerosene when the existing supply was depleted.

Iris's mind drifted as she warmed herself by the woodstove. She was constantly daydreaming of methods to make money. Money to help her family make it through the trying times.

The problem was you needed money to make money. Everybody knew that. And money was something the Jansen's lacked.

Iris and Sarah shared a small bedroom. Their beds were side-by-side. That night, as they turned in, Sarah's stomach rumbled. Iris heard the rumbling from her bed. Then Iris's stomach rumbled even louder. The sisters burst out in laughter, a short but welcome reprieve.

*****

Sarah made coffee the following morning while Iris went out to the cider press in the barn. Iris emptied a bucket of apples into the cider press and placed a jar below the spout at the bottom of the press. Then she cranked the handle to compress the apples. It wasn't long until the jar was full of cider.

The sisters walked to the farm stand together that morning. Iris carried the jar of cider; Sarah carried the coffee pot. The temperature hovered at nineteen degrees, and the girls shivered as a frigid gust of wind cut through their hand-me-down jackets.

When they arrived at the stand, Iris got a fire going in the woodstove and Sarah placed the coffee pot on top of it. Then they waited.

Two vehicles—an old Model A and a Buick Roadster—passed by just before noon. But neither one stopped. The sisters were growing restless from inactivity. They needed a distraction, something to make the endless waiting a little more bearable. Iris came up with an idea. "We should decorate."

"Decorate?"

"Yes. We should decorate the stand for Christmas."

"With what?" Sarah asked.

Iris thought for a few moments. Then she said: "I'll be back in a jiffy."

Iris headed out back to the barn. Once there, she grabbed a piece of bailing wire, a pair of brush clippers, a spool of string, and a pair of wire cutters. Then she walked over to the house and retrieved a length of red ribbon she had been saving. Iris brought the supplies to the farmstand and placed them on the wooden table that had previously been used to display vegetables.

Sarah looked at the items and furrowed her brow, but before she could say anything, Iris picked up the brush cutters and headed outside again. She returned ten minutes later with an armload of pine boughs.

"Okay, I give up," Sarah said. "What are we doing?"

"You'll see soon enough."

Sarah watched as her sister shaped a piece of bailing wire it into a circle. Iris overlapped the ends of the bailing wire and bound them with a length of string she had cut from the spool. The end result was a circular frame about twelve inches in diameter.

Next, she cut several more lengths of string. Then she picked up a pine bough and fastened it to the bailing wire frame with a piece of string. After the bough was fastened to the frame, she repeated the process and secured another bough over the first one.

"A wreath," Sarah observed.

Iris nodded. "You can decorate it," she said. "You should be able to find some pinecones out back."

Sarah beamed. "Be right back."

*****

Iris was securing the last bough to the wreath when Sarah returned with a dozen pinecones. "You can cut small pieces of string from the spool and use them to secure the pinecones to the wreath," Iris advised.

Iris cut a length of red ribbon and fashioned it into a bow. She fastened the bow to the wreath as Sarah tied pinecones to it.

The sisters stepped back and admired their work when they finished. Then Iris said, "Let's hang the wreath outside on the front door."

"Yes. Maybe it will attract some business."

"I hope so. Let's make a wreath for the window, too."

*****

The second wreath was much fuller than the first one. The sisters had learned from their mistakes. They used twice as many pine boughs on the second wreath. And they secured pinecones and a ribbon bow to the wreath with thin wire rather than string.

"I think we should place *this* wreath on the door," Sarah stated as they completed the second wreath. "The other one can go on the barn."

Iris nodded in agreement.

Later that afternoon, as the sun began to edge down over the mountains, Iris and Sarah were getting ready to close the stand. Then they heard the rumble of a distant vehicle, a truck heading north. They decided to wait.

Five minutes later, an old Ford flatbed truck pulled to a stop in front of the stand. The truck was rust-pocked, and its paint was so faded there was no telling what its original color had been.

Iris and Sarah watched through the farmstand's window as a man disembarked from the driver's side of the cab. A blond-haired boy was asleep on the passenger side of the cab. He appeared to be Iris's age.

The man walked over to the farmstand and knocked on the door. Iris opened the door. The man was enormous. He was barrel-chested and stood well over six feet tall. He held a thermos in his left hand. "Good evening, girls," he greeted. "Your sign caught my eye. We've been on the road all day. Sure could use some hot coffee."

This sisters' spirits immediately lifted. The wait had been worthwhile for once.

Sarah walked over to the woodstove and retrieved the coffee pot. "Would you like me to fill the thermos?"

"That would be swell. We've got a ways to go yet." He handed the thermos to Sarah. Then he moved over to the woodstove and warmed his hands while Sarah filled the thermos with coffee. "Your sign said you have cider, too?"

Iris beamed. "Yes. Would you like some?"

"My boy sure would enjoy some cider when he wakes up."

Iris retrieved the jar of cider from the shelf at the back of the stand and showed it to the man. "That will make Gerry's day," he said.

"Do you have a cup or a container for cider?" Iris inquired. "We need to keep the jar. It's one of the few we have left."

"No, but tell you what. We'll be passing by here again in three days on our return trip. If you could let us borrow the jar until then, we'll drop it off. I might just need some more coffee at that time."

"That would be fine," Iris hesitantly replied as she handed the man the precious jar of cider.

"Splendid. Appreciate it, young lady."

"Where are you headed?" Sarah inquired as she topped off the man's thermos.

"Home. Canada. We're heading up for a load of trees."

"Christmas trees?"

"That's right. Some people in the city still have the means to purchase them, if you can believe it. Business is nothing like it was in years past by any means, but we manage to sell some trees. My oldest boy is back in the city right now tending our tree lot."

"Which city?" Iris asked.

"The big one. New York."

Sarah handed the man the thermos. He removed the thermos's cap and took a long pull of coffee. Then the wreath on the front door caught his eye. "Where did you get the wreath?" he asked as he screwed the lid back on the thermos. "Was it made locally?"

"We made it," Sarah boasted.

The man paused for a moment. Then he said: "Folks in the city—the ones that buy our trees—sometimes they inquire about wreaths. They ask if we have any wreaths for sale. But we don't. If you girls could make a batch of wreaths similar to this one, there might be an opportunity to sell a few. I'd be glad to try to sell some wreaths for you."

Iris and Sarah exchanged glances. "Really?"

"Sure. I can't promise you they'd sell. But we could give it a try."

"You mean like a partnership?" Iris asked.

"That's right," the man said. "We can work out the details later."

"You have a deal."

"Excellent, girls. Now, how much do I owe you for the coffee and cider?"

Iris thought for a moment. "Well, we charge three cents for a cup of coffee. And your thermos probably holds about four cups. So that would be twelve cents. And cider is five cents a cup. There's probably two cups of cider in the jar. So that would be another ten cents—twenty-two cents total."

The man reached into his pocket and withdrew a fifty-cent piece. He handed it to Iris. "Here you go."

Iris glanced at the coin. "I'm sorry. We can only accept the exact amount. We don't have any change."

The man smiled. "I'm not asking for any change. See you girls in three days."

"Thanks mister!"

"Thank *you*."

The sisters ran up to the house to tell their parents about their good fortune as soon as the truck pulled away from the farmstand. Their mother was in the kitchen with the baby when they arrived. Sarah showed her mother the fifty-cent piece. "We had a good day!"

Her mother's eyes were suddenly watery as she looked at the coin, and her face creased in a smile. "Oh, my! That's wonderful, girls! Just wonderful. What a godsend. We are going to have meat on our plates tonight. There's still time to make it to Bryce's before they close."

*****

Bryce's General Store was a twenty-minute walk from the house. The hanging bells on the store's front door announced their arrival when Iris and Sarah stepped into the establishment. Old man Bryce was behind the cash register. "Evening, girls."

"Hello, Mr. Bryce."

"Let me know if I can help you find anything."

"Thanks, sir."

Five minutes later, the sisters placed the provisions they had selected on the counter. In all, there was a loaf of bread, a dozen eggs, one pound of sugar, a can of beans, one pound of hamburger, and a pound of frankfurters. Iris handed the proprietor the fifty-cent piece. He placed it in the cash register's change drawer and handed her change: three cents—just enough for a newspaper. Iris bought one for her father. It would be a luxury.

*****

Iris and Sarah were up at dawn the following morning. Sarah made coffee while Iris went out to the cider press to make a jar of cider. They headed to the farmstand fifteen minutes later. When they arrived at the stand, they stoked the coals in the woodstove and added a few pieces of firewood.

Once the fire was roaring in the woodstove, the girls got down to business. Iris cut sections of bailing wire and fashioned them into circular frames. Sarah went outside and gathered pine boughs and pinecones. She piled them on the floor beside the woodstove when she returned ten minutes later.

The sisters worked together, fastening the pine boughs to bailing wire frames. It was slow going at first, but soon they slipped into a comfortable rhythm.

By noon, they had completed four wreaths. They crafted six more wreaths that afternoon. The next day, they crafted ten more.

The day after that Sarah brewed the pot of coffee while Iris worked the cider press out in the barn. The sisters headed over to the farmstand earlier than usual that day. They wanted to be prepared when the man and his son arrived. The sisters crafted five more wreaths while they waited.

*****

The old Ford flatbed truck pulled up to the farmstand just before noon. The blond-haired boy was awake this time. He followed his father inside. "Morning, girls!" the man boomed as he and his son stepped into the farmstand. "Wow! Look at that," he remarked, taking in the neatly stacked piles of wreaths beside the door. "You two have been busy, I see."

The boy was holding the jar his father had borrowed. He handed the jar to Iris. "Thanks."

Iris blushed. Then she handed the boy the jar of cider she had made that morning. "Here you go."

The boy looked at Iris. "Thank you."

Iris blushed once more. She noticed the boy's eyes were dark blue like his father's.

"Would you like some coffee?" Sarah asked the boy's father.

"Yes, please," the man replied. "I've been looking forward to it." He handed Sarah his thermos.

Iris and the boy exchanged glances as Sarah filled the thermos. When the thermos was full, Sarah handed it to the boy's father. "Here you go."

"Much obliged, young lady." The man handed Sarah a fifty-cent piece.

"We still don't have change," Sarah told him.

"I'm not looking for any. Happy holidays!"

"Thanks!"

The man glanced over at the pile of wreaths. "Well, let's load the wreaths on the truck, Gerry."

"Uh... we haven't talked about pricing yet," Iris pointed out.

The man scratched his chin. Then he said, "I think fifty-cents per wreath would be reasonable. We could always lower the price if there are no takers."

"Um… I meant we haven't talked about our pricing *arrangement*," Iris clarified.

"Oh," the man replied. "Well, I think a twenty percent cut would be fair enough."

"You mean we'd receive twenty percent of the sales?" Iris asked. "Ten cents for each wreath sold?"

The man shook his head. "No, *our* cut would be twenty percent. *Your* cut would be eighty percent. You two did all the work after all."

Iris and Sarah exchanged glances. "Thank you! That's more than fair."

"Thank *you*," the man returned. "Let's load the wreaths on the truck, Gerry."

"We'll help," Iris offered.

"That would be swell."

The battered Ford flatbed truck pulled away from the farmstand ten minutes later, the wreaths nestled in among a load of freshly-cut Christmas trees. "We'll be back on Christmas Eve," the man hollered as the truck pulled onto the road and headed south.

The sisters ran home. They gave the fifty-cent piece to their mother. Her eyes widened when she saw the coin. "What a blessing! We'll tuck it away for now. There are still some provisions left over from your last trip to the general store."

*****

In the days that followed, Iris and Sarah continued their vigil at the farmstand. They brought a pot of coffee to the stand each morning, but they no longer offered cider for sale. The apple barrel was almost empty. Iris wanted to be sure there were enough apples for a jar of cider on Christmas Eve. The blond-haired boy would need some cider for his long journey. The boy had been in her thoughts as of late.

*****

A cold front pushed in from the west two days before Christmas; the temperature plummeted. Iris and Sarah took turns braving the elements to obtain firewood to keep the woodstove going at the farmstand. And they made three more wreaths before they ran out of bailing wire.

The wreaths they crafted now were a vast improvement over their earlier attempts. The sisters took their time, carefully securing pine boughs to the circular bailing wire frames. They decorated each wreath with pine cones as well as walnut shells now, hoping to sell the wreaths to passersby. But business was just as dismal as before. Nobody stopped by the farm stand.

*****

Iris and Sarah arrived at the farmstand earlier than usual on Christmas Eve morning. The boy's father hadn't said what time he and the boy would be stopping by on their return trip. The sisters did not want to miss them.

Sarah brought the usual pot of coffee, and Iris brought a jar of cider she had pressed from the last of the apples. They got a fire going in the woodstove and placed the coffee pot atop it. Then the sisters played solitaire to pass the time.

*****

The old Ford flatbed truck pulled up in front of the farmstand late that afternoon, just as the sun began to descend behind the mountains. Iris and Sarah watched anxiously as the boy and his father disembarked from the cab. The man was carrying his thermos.

"Good afternoon, girls!" he shouted as he and the boy entered the farmstand.

"Good afternoon," Iris and Sarah said in unison.

The man placed his thermos on the table. Then he went over to the woodstove and warmed his hands. The boy was carrying an empty jar. He handed it to Iris. "Thanks," he said.

"You're welcome," Iris smiled. She handed him the jar of cider she had made that morning. "Don't worry about the jar this time," she said. "You can return it next year."

The boy grinned. "Okay. Thanks."

A few moments later the man pulled a billfold from his back pocket and extracted ten dollars. "Well," he announced triumphantly, "we sold twenty wreaths—at fifty cents each." He handed Iris ten one dollar bills.

Iris thought her legs were going to give out. She'd never held or even seen that much money. "Th-thanks," she stammered. Visions of what the money could buy loomed in the forefront of her thoughts. But then she realized the man had overpaid her. She peeled two dollar bills from the money and attempted to hand back, but he held up his hands in refusal.

"This is yours," Iris told him. "We owe you twenty percent of the sales."

"No you don't," the man replied.

"Huh?"

"We didn't need a twenty percent cut after all."

"I don't understand."

The man smiled. "We sold more trees thanks to those wreaths you girls made. You see, we strung the wreaths up on a wire at the front of the lot. They caught some attention and brought us more business than expected. If it were not for the wreaths, we surely would not have sold as many trees."

"Are you sure?"

"Yes. There's no doubt about it."

"Thanks!"

"Thank *you*. Oh," the man said, reaching into his jacket pocket. "This is for you." He extracted a solid crystal star-shaped Christmas ornament and handed it to Iris. It was about the size of a silver dollar. The star was perfectly symmetrical, and all of its edges were finely beveled. The ornament had obviously been crafted by an artisan.

Iris was awestruck. She looked up at the man with questioning eyes. He smiled.

"When we packed up to leave this morning," he explained, "a woman approached us. I recognized her. There was a soup kitchen across the street from the tree lot. There was always a long line there. The

94

woman and her four children were in that line every day no matter what the weather was like. Sometimes they stood in line for hours.

"Anyhow, we had a dozen trees and five wreaths left when we were getting ready to close up and head home. The woman inquired about the remaining trees and wreaths. I told her they were no longer of use to us, and that she was welcome to them. I thought you wouldn't mind. It wasn't like we could sell the trees and wreaths elsewhere. I told her the lot was leased until midnight and that she was welcome to stay until then.

"I don't think I've ever made anyone as happy as I did at that moment. The woman cried. She thanked me profusely. I wished her luck and was about to hop in the truck to head home when she gently grabbed my arm and said, 'I can't pay you. But I have something for you.'

"I told her it was not necessary. But she didn't listen. She reached into a hidden pocket in her tattered jacket and extracted the ornament. Then she handed it to me. I tried to give it back to her, but she refused to take it. 'I have another,' she said. 'It was part of a set. I insist that you take it.'

"I tried once more to return the ornament to her, but once again she refused to take it back. We had a lot of miles to cover and didn't have time to linger—so I thanked the woman, put the ornament in my pocket, and hopped in the truck. Before we pulled out of the lot, I handed her the sandwiches I had made for the trip. She accepted them. 'Godspeed to you and your family!' she called out as we drove away."

Iris stared at the ornament in the palm of her hand. "I can't accept this," she said. "The woman gave it *you*. You should keep it."

The man shrugged. "It's of no use to me."

"Are you sure?"

"I am."

"That's very kind of you. Thank you so much."

Sarah picked up the man's thermos and carried it over to the woodstove. Iris and the boy exchanged glances as Sarah lifted the coffee pot from the woodstove and filled the thermos. After the thermos was full, Sarah handed it to the boy's father. "Here you go."

The man tipped his hat. "Much obliged. It's been nice chatting and doing business with you girls, but we'd best be moving on. We've got a lot of miles to cover yet. We'll plan to stop by on our way south next year—the first week of December. We can do the same arrangement with the wreaths if you like."

Iris and Sarah beamed. "We'll have a batch of wreaths ready!"

"Splendid, girls. Happy holidays."

"Happy holidays!"

The boy started to follow his father out the door, but then he stopped and turned around. He looked at Iris. "Merry Christmas."

Iris smiled. "Merry Christmas. See you next year."

"You can count on it."

Iris and Sarah watched as the truck pulled away and disappeared in the distance.

"We're rich!" Sarah yelled.

Iris smiled at her younger sister. "Let's go. We have some shopping to do."

*****

They grabbed a wagon from the barn—the one they used to haul crops from the garden. The two of them took turns pulling the wagon down the road. They sang carols as they made their way to the general store.

Mr. Bryce was in his customary place behind the cash register when the sisters arrived. "Afternoon, girls."

"Hello, Mr. Bryce."

The old proprietor raised his eyebrows when he saw Iris select a ten-pound ham from the meat section and place it on the counter. But the ham was not to be the girls' only purchase. Iris and Sarah placed other items on the counter, too: a loaf of bread, a quart of milk, half a pound of butter, a dozen eggs, two oranges, a slab of bacon, a tin of baking powder, one pound of sugar, vanilla extract, a jar of peanut butter, and a sack of flour.

Mr. Bryce rang up the items. The total came to $3.25. Iris paid him, and Mr. Bryce bid the sisters *Merry Christmas* as they carried the items outside to the wagon.

"A Merry Christmas to you, too, Mr. Bryce."

Nightfall was approaching, and the temperature was quickly dropping, but the sisters didn't feel the cold. As they pulled the wagon home, the two of them rambled on excitedly about their good fortune. They talked about the Christmas cookies and cakes they'd bake. And there was mention of pancakes, eggs, and bacon for breakfast on Christmas morning.

The sisters talked nonstop—until they neared the widow's house. Only one room was illuminated in the old house. Iris pictured the widow and her five children huddled around a kerosene lantern. Perhaps the

97

widow was reading to her children. Their Christmas would not be a merry one. The same was true for the steeplejack and the elderly couple down the road.

When they got home, their mother was upstairs ironing, and the baby was napping. Iris and Sarah brought the groceries into the kitchen and placed the ham, bacon, milk, and butter in the ice box. Then Iris looked at Sarah and said, "We need to go back to the general store."

Sarah seemed to read her sister's mind. She nodded. "Yes. Let's go."

Before heading off to the general store, Iris grabbed three burlap bags from the barn and placed them in the wagon. Sarah retrieved the last three wreaths they had made at the farmstand and placed them in the wagon, too. Then the sisters headed back to Bryce's General Store. The sun had gone down, and a harvest moon illuminated the nightscape. They had no trouble navigating their way to the store.

"Didn't expect to see you girls back so soon," Mr. Bryce stated when Iris and Sarah stepped into the store.

"Hello, again, Mr. Bryce. We're not done shopping yet."

"You know where everything is, girls. But let me know if I can be of help."

"Thanks, Mr. Bryce."

The old proprietor looked on with curiosity as Iris and Sarah carried items to the counter. By the time they had finished shopping, there were five quarts of milk, three hams, cans of soup and beans, loaves of bread, slabs of bacon, flour, sugar, oranges, and three boxes of eggs on the counter.

Intuition told the old proprietor that the items on the counter were not for the Jansen family. After the girls paid for the groceries, he said, "Hold on a minute." Then he picked up a paper sack and filled it with licorice and stick candy—sassafras, peppermint, butterscotch, and cinnamon. He handed the sack of candy to Iris along with three tins of ginger snaps.

"Thanks, Mr. Bryce. That's mighty kind of you."

"No girls, it's mighty kind of *you*. God bless and happy holidays to you and your family."

"And to you, Mr. Bryce. See you next year."

Iris and Sarah filled the three burlap sacks with groceries and tied the top of each sack with a piece of red ribbon. Then they placed the sacks in the wagon and pulled the wagon down the road.

When they reached the widow's home, they placed a sack of groceries, a wreath, and three quarts of milk on the front stoop. They also left the bag of candy that Mr. Bryce had provided. Then they knocked on the front door three times and shouted: "Christmas delivery!"

After that, the sisters pulled the wagon to the steeplejack's shack and left a sack of food, a wreath, and a quart of milk by his front door. They knocked on his door three times and shouted: "Christmas delivery!"

They left the last sack of groceries, wreath, and quart of milk on the front porch at the elderly couple's place. Once again they knocked on the door three times, and shouted "Christmas delivery." Then the sisters headed home to help their mother prepare for Christmas.

Chapter 19

A few moments passed in silence after my grandmother finished telling the story. Then she reached into the small wooden box and extracted one of the two objects inside it. She carefully removed the tissue paper from the object. Underneath the wrapping was an ornament—a crystal star.

"The ornament from the story," I guessed.

My grandmother nodded. "It is indeed." She carefully handed me the crystal star ornament. It was very ornate and truly unique; I had never seen anything like it. As alluded to in my grandmother's story, the ornament had clearly been crafted by an artisan. The beveled edges of the star's five points glistened, and the lights on the Christmas tree reflected in the crystal. I admired the ornament for a few minutes. Then I attempted to hand it back to my grandmother. But she raised her hands in refusal. "You keep it," she said, "for your Christmas Tin."

"Are you sure?"

"Yes. It's time I passed it along. Perhaps you can share the story with Mariana, Anna, Paul—and your grandchildren, some day."

I gave my grandmother a kiss on the cheek. "I'll do that. Thanks, Grandma."

I gently placed the ornament in the Christmas Tin. Then I returned to the couch and took a seat beside my grandmother. She had closed the lid on the small wooden box, I noted.

"Did you ever see the boy again?" I inquired.

My grandmother smiled. "Yes…I married him. The boy was your grandfather."

I nodded. "That was quite a story."

My grandmother flashed a smile. "It's one of my favorites, I must confess."

"So…are you going to unwrap the other object in the box?"

My grandmother hesitated. "No. Your grandfather needs to tell the story behind that one—if you can get him to talk about it. It's his. He brought it back from the war. And you know how he's not one to talk about his wartime experience."

This I knew. I had asked my grandfather about the war when I was a kid. But he didn't say much. I recall him talking about cold weather. And he mentioned something about having to wait in long lines for chow. That was about it.

I had asked my father if my grandfather ever told him any stories about his wartime experience. Dad told me he just mentioned a few tidbits. Things you didn't usually find in history books. He said my grandfather mentioned how K-ration boxes were useful as tinder. He told him how the bolt on his rifle froze up because of the extreme weather. He also talked about a long ride in the back of an open truck, one of many in a convoy he referred to as the Red Ball Express. But my father told me that my grandfather never talked about the fighting. Dad said my grandfather was awarded a Bronze Star and a Silver Star, but he wasn't privy to the stories behind them. I knew there was little chance that my grandfather would talk about the mysterious object in the box.

"Well," I said. "I have a few more floorboards to replace."

"I'll let you get back to it. Your grandfather and I are very grateful you're here, Jesse."

"I'm glad to be here," I replied. "And I sure do enjoy your cooking, Grandma. Are you baking more pumpkin bread today?"

"I am. Actually, I'm planning to make a delivery later this afternoon and am hoping you might be able to drive me."

"I am at your service."

"Thanks, sweetheart."

*****

I was nailing in a floorboard a half hour later when my cell phone rang.

Caller ID announced it was Wendy. I answered. "Hey, Wendy."

"Hi, boss." Wendy sounded upbeat.

"How goes it?"

"Well," she began, "things are kind of…interesting at the moment. There have been some *developments* since we last spoke."

"Oh?"

"Yes. Steve Hartnick, the investor who owns the twenty-four unit office building, isn't going to renew his management contract with Central New England Real Estate Group. He just called this morning."

"No kidding. Does Steve plan to self-manage his building?"

"He didn't say. But he *did* say he would like to meet with you. He asked where you are."

"Is that so?"

"Yes, and there's more. Steve is not the only one who wants to meet with you. The other two investors—Jake Templeton and Ike Cauldwelle—want to meet with you, too."

"That's interesting. When did Jake and Ike call?"

"This morning. About fifteen minutes after Steve called."

"Did they say what they wanted to meet with me about?"

"No. But I can tell you that it looks like Jake and Ike are not planning to renew their management contracts either. They have not signed them yet, anyhow. My hunch is the three of them talked at the monthly Chamber of Commerce breakfast and compared notes. You know how they get together at those breakfast meetings and talk business. It sounds like Steve is the spokesperson. He asked if you might be available to meet with the three of them at lunch on Monday. They'll be at Nick's Diner at noon."

"Well," I replied. "I'm up in Vermont right now. The cell phone reception is a little unpredictable in the mountains. Wendy, could I impose on you to let Steve know I'll join him, Jake, and Ike for lunch on Monday?

"Will do, boss. It will be a pleasure."

"Thanks, Wendy."

"No problemo. Oh, one more thing. Gisueppi Moretti called yesterday. He *really* wants to talk with you. He said he'd like to invite you to dinner next week."

"Hmmm. Wendy, I hate to ask, but do you think you could also call Gisueppi and let him know that Monday night would work well for dinner if he's available?"

"You betcha. I'll be in touch."

104

"Thanks so much again, Wendy."

"Glad to be of service."

I mulled things over for a few minutes after Wendy's call. I wondered about the agenda for the upcoming lunch meeting with Steve, Jake, and Ike. All three investors had always been professional and were a pleasure to work with. I'd do my best to provide any advice or direction that I could. I owed them that much.

I also thought about Gisueppi and looked forward to having dinner with him. I liked the man, had always enjoyed his company. Gisueppi surely wanted to ask my advice about some matter. I would do my best to help him as well.

I called Mariana, but got her voicemail. I left her a message indicating that I was coming home this weekend. I mentioned the lunch meeting on Monday and let her know I wouldn't be home for dinner on Monday night. Then I went inside to break the news to my grandmother. She was removing a loaf of pumpkin bread from the oven when I caught up with her. "I'm sorry, Grandma. But my stay is going to be cut short. I'm going to need to head home this weekend."

My grandmother smiled and placed the pumpkin bread on the kitchen counter. "I'm surprised you've been able to stay this long. We've treasured every minute of your stay."

"As have I, Grandma. Thanks for having me."

I hadn't told her about my employment situation. But I felt like talking about it at that moment and brought her up to date. My grandmother had always been a great listener.

"What a foolish company," she said of Central New England Real Estate Group after I filled her in. "How a company can do business like that is beyond me. But, I'll tell you something, good things can result from bad situations. Mark my words."

"Thanks, Grandma." I found some solace in her words.

"Do you still have time to help me make a delivery this afternoon?"

"You bet. I just have a few more floorboards to nail in. Then I'm all yours."

*****

I nailed the last floorboard in place just before two o'clock. Then I put my tools away and stepped into the farmhouse. My grandmother was in the kitchen placing tin foil over a loaf of warm pumpkin bread when I caught up with her. "The porch is all set," I informed her.

"Thanks, sweetheart. Let me just finish wrapping this up, and we'll head out. Eleanor's place is just down the road."

We stepped outside five minutes later and headed over to the SUV. My grandmother intertwined her left arm in my right as we walked across the front yard. She was bundled up in her wool coat and draped around her neck was a red and green woolen scarf.

Five miles after pulling out of the driveway, my grandmother said, "Turn right just beyond that mailbox up ahead."

I did as she said, and we headed up a gravel driveway that twisted through a stand of maple trees. At the end of the driveway was a small stone-fronted Victorian farmhouse with a slate roof.

An elderly African American woman was collecting eggs in a small chicken coop beside the house when we pulled up. She was a buxom woman, slightly shorter than my grandmother. Her face creased in a grin when she saw my grandmother disembark from the SUV. "Hello there, Iris!"

"Hello, Eleanor. You are hardier than me. I've been inside the house all day. This weather is too cold for this time of year."

"That it is. That it is."

We made our way over to Eleanor. She placed her egg basket on the ground as we reached her, and my grandmother embraced her.

"This is my grandson, Jesse."

"Hello there, Jesse. You've got some of your grandfather in you, I see."

"Nice to meet you, Eleanor. I've been told that before."

A gust of wind chilled the three of us just then.

"Good Lord," Eleanor remarked. "Let's go inside and warm up. Get some hot tea in us."

"That sounds heavenly," my grandmother replied.

I picked up the egg basket.

"Thank you, Jesse."

"My pleasure."

Eleanor and my grandmother chatted on the way to the house. I trailed behind them, marveling at the snow-capped fields and overgrown orchard that back dropped the small homestead.

When we entered the house, I took in the wide pinewood floorboards in the front foyer. Beyond the foyer was a living room with a stone hearth. To the right of the hearth was a Christmas tree decorated with handcrafted paper ornaments—angels.

"Have a seat," Eleanor said, motioning to the living room sofa. "I'll get the tea going."

"Jesse," my grandmother said. "I left the pumpkin bread in the car. Could you brave the elements and go get it?"

"You bet. Be right back."

I went out to the SUV to get the pumpkin bread. When I returned to the house, my grandmother and Eleanor were in the kitchen. They were engaged in pleasant conversation when I stepped into the kitchen with the pumpkin bread.

There was a coziness to the kitchen with its birch cabinets, soapstone counter, and old fashioned white porcelain sink. On top of the counter was a vintage canister set: coffee, tea, sugar, and flour. An old Morton Salt sign was tacked to the wall above the canisters, adding to the ambiance.

A picture window on the kitchen's far wall provided a view of a backyard garden and an expansive snow-covered hay field.

"Here you go," I said, placing the pumpkin bread on the counter.

Eleanor smiled. "Why, thank you, Jesse. I'll warm this up and we can snack on it in the living room with our tea. Could I trouble you to build a fire in the hearth?"

My face creased in a grin. "I'm on it."

I made my way down the hall to the living room and walked over to the hearth. There was a basket of kindling next to the hearth. Beside the kindling was a box of split firewood. It didn't take long to get a fire started.

Once the fire was going, I meandered around the room. I took in the Christmas tree and the simple, but intriguing, paper angel ornaments that adorned it.

Then my focus shifted to the mantel over the hearth. I made my way over to it. Resting on the mantel was a framed sepia tone photograph of two soldiers.

"The one on the left was my Harold," Eleanor announced, startling me. I hadn't heard her enter the room.

"World War II?" I asked.

Eleanor nodded. She was holding a plate of sliced pumpkin bread. "The soldier next to Harold was his brother, Melvin. They were with the 92nd Infantry Division."

"Where did they serve?"

"Italy. Melvin did not return from the war, but Harold made it home. He lived a long life. Just passed on two years ago."

My grandmother stepped into the room just then carrying a tray. On the tray were three cups of steaming tea. "Harold and your grandfather were great friends," she interjected.

"Indeed they were," Eleanor confirmed. "Now, let's enjoy this pumpkin bread."

Eleanor placed the plate of pumpkin bread on a cherrywood side table, and my grandmother set the tray down beside it.

On one side of the table was a wooden ladder-back chair with a cane seat. On the other side was an old Sears, Roebuck & Company couch. Eleanor and my grandmother sat on the couch. I opted for the chair.

We snacked on warm pumpkin bread and chatted for a few minutes as we waited for the tea to cool. Then my grandmother said, "Jesse, I told Eleanor about your Christmas Tin."

"I've always been partial to the holidays," Eleanor claimed.

I couldn't help but smile. "Me, too."

"I wouldn't mind seeing that Christmas Tin of yours," Eleanor remarked.

"I wish I had thought to bring it. I'd be glad to show it to you."

"If you're okay with leaving the tin with us until Christmas," my grandmother spoke up, "I could show it to Eleanor tomorrow. We'll be getting together over at our place tomorrow afternoon to craft some gifts for the Christmas bazaar.

"You got it."

Eleanor smiled. Then she looked over at the Christmas tree. She seemed lost in thought for a few moments.

I glanced at the tree, too. The paper angels contrasted nicely with the Frasier fir's green needles. There was something striking about the simple handcrafted ornaments. There were a dozen of them in all.

"Do you like my angels?" Eleanor asked.

"I do. They're unique. Did you make them?"

Eleanor grinned. "I just made the first one. My great grandchildren crafted the others. I got them started. They are quick learners."

"Is there a story behind the angel ornaments?"

Eleanor sipped her tea. Then she slowly placed her cup on the tray atop the cherry wood table.

"Yes, there is, in fact," she replied. "An old story from another time."

My eyebrows lifted. "How far back?"

"Before my day. The story goes back generations—to when my great- grandmother was a girl."

My interest was piqued.

"Would you like to hear the story?" Eleanor asked.

"I would love to hear it."

"Do you have a little time?"

I looked over at my grandmother. She smiled and gave me a nod.

"I sure do."

Eleanor lifted her cup and took another sip of tea. Then she sat back and looked over at the Christmas tree again. There was a distant look in her eyes as she began to tell the story that she had first heard during in her youth...

Chapter 20

December 12, 1858

Eleven-year-old Hannah woke as the cabin's door creaked open. It was well past midnight, nearly dawn. The door opened further. Hannah could make out a man in the doorway. Her father; he was illuminated in the moonlight.

Her father shut the door gently behind him and quietly made his way over to the sleeping pallet that he and Hannah's mother—Clarissa—shared. He was asleep within minutes.

Hannah lay awake on the pallet she shared with her seven-year-old brother, Edson. He was sleeping peacefully, but Hannah knew she would not be able to fall back to sleep. Her mind was preoccupied. She could never fall asleep after her father returned from his Saturday evening forays.

Her father had been quietly slipping away from the cabin on Saturday evenings since August. He always returned just before sunup on Sunday. Hannah knew what he was doing. She had overheard her parents talking about it a few weeks before. Her parents had talked in hushed voices late that night as Hannah and Edson lay nearby. They didn't know that Hannah heard them talking. Hannah was old enough to know she couldn't tell anyone about the secret. None of the other slaves could know about it. Not yet. She didn't even tell Edson.

Hannah didn't know where her father traveled on Saturday evenings, but she knew the direction of his route: north. He had been traveling a little further north each week, getting to know the lay of the land beyond the plantation.

It was dangerous to venture off the plantation. If patrollers caught a slave off the plantation without a pass, there would be severe consequences. But risk was unavoidable for a slave looking to make a run for freedom. Gaining familiarity with the woodlands and countryside they would be crossing would give the family an edge, or so Hannah's father hoped. He kept an eye out for hiding places and food sources on his Saturday evening forays. He also searched for water. Streams, rivers, and swamps. Water could mask scent and throw bloodhounds off course.

Hannah knew the date they would leave: Christmas Eve. She had overheard it when listening to her parents' conversation that night. The slaves on the plantation had Christmas day off.

For those that toiled in the fields from sunup to sundown, six days a week, Christmas provided a much needed break. It was a time of merriment. With the exception of Sundays, it was the only day of the year that the field slaves didn't need to worry about the overseer's whip. All of the slaves looked forward to the much needed day off that Christmas provided.

This year, Christmas fell on Saturday. The slaves would have a two-day reprieve from the fields. And Hannah's family would have a two-day head start on their journey north. It wouldn't be much of a head start—they would be on foot and the patrollers and slave catchers travelled on horseback—but it was the best they could hope for.

Two days later, Edson was playing marbles by the well with the other slave boys when a high-end horse carriage pulled up in front of the big house. A heavyset man disembarked from the carriage. He was clad in white linen trousers and a scarlet tail coat. Under his coat he wore a pressed cotton shirt and a dark silk damask vest.

"That's massa's cousin," one of the boys said.

"He from here 'bouts?" another boy asked.

"Further south. Heard he owns a plantation bigger 'n this one."

The boys watched the man as he made his way up the expansive granite steps in front of the big house. From the scowl on his face, he didn't appear to be a humble man.

Missus came out to greet the man. He removed his top hat and bowed. Then the two of them stepped inside the big house. The boys shifted their focus back to their game of marbles.

That night, as Hannah's family was eating supper—corn pone— someone knocked on the door. Hannah's father got up from the table—a weathered board placed over two wooden barrels. He made his way over to the door and peered through the cracks.

A smile took shape on his face when he saw it was Talitha. Talitha worked in the kitchen at the big house. Sometimes she brought the family leftovers.

When Hannah's father opened the door, Talitha quickly stepped inside the small one-room cabin. It was as if she were afraid she was being followed. She wasn't carrying food this time. And there was a look on the woman's face that Hannah had never seen before, a nervous, worried look. Talitha was shaking.

Hannah's mother got up and walked over to console her friend. "What's wrong, Talitha?" she asked softly.

Talitha wiped a tear from her face with the back of her hand. Then she looked at Hannah's mother. "I tried to come earlier," she said, her voice panic-stricken. "But missus was lingering in the kitchen tonight...I have news...Bad news." Talitha's eyes were moist.

Hannah listened intently. The family was on edge as Talitha filled them in. The massa's cousin was visiting at the big house. The man had a plantation in the deep South. He had been unkind to the slaves that worked in the big house. He belittled them for small infractions, mentioned the punishment the field slaves on his plantation received for far lesser infractions.

Talitha stopped and wiped away another tear. Then she got to the root of her worry. "He came to purchase a slave from massa," she said, her voice cracking. "A woman."

Hannah's heart went out to Talitha. Being separated from one's family and friends was every slave's greatest fear on the plantation. Talitha's cooking skills were no secret. All of the guests at the big house commented on her cooking. And because of her culinary skills, she was being taken away.

Hannah's mother embraced Talitha. Tears welled in her eyes now too. "Oh heavens, Talitha."

Talitha gently pulled away. She looked up at Hannah's mother through watery eyes. Then she said, "It's not what you think...I'm not the one he wants...It's *you* he wants, Clarissa."

116

Hannah's mother slumped to the floor. The small one-room cabin was suddenly silent. Hannah's heart raced. She could feel her blood pulsating in her ears. Her biggest fear had come true. She had worried about this happening since she was old enough to understand about the bonds of slavery. Hannah had long worried that her mother's beauty would be her downfall.

Hannah had tried to banish the thought from her mind over the years. Her mother did not work in the big house, after all. She was not readily visible to those who visited the plantation; Hannah's mother worked in the fields—away from the eyes of guests and slave traders, and yet this vulgar man had found her.

A few moments passed in silence as the shock set in. Then Hannah's father asked, "When does massa's cousin head south?"

Talitha cleared her throat. "The day after tomorrow—Thursday. In the morning. After breakfast."

Hannah's father's shoulders slumped.

Talitha wiped more tears from her eyes. "I must be gettin' back to the big house. I will stop by again tomorrow night."

*****

Talitha stopped by the cabin the following evening as promised. When she neared the cabin and didn't see the glow of a grease lamp through the cracks in the door, she knew the cabin was empty. The family had fled.

Chapter 21

There had been no time for good-byes. Hannah and her parents worked in the fields for twelve hours that day. Edson had been instructed to remain in the cabin for the day. When Hannah and her parents returned to the cabin at sundown, they moved quickly.

Everyone pulled on extra layers of clothing and threadbare winter coats. Then Hannah's father removed a gunny sack that had been secreted in the wood pile beside the hearth. Inside the sack was a homemade knife, a drinking gourd, a spool of thread with a needle, a small cast iron pan, a piece of rawhide, a length of rope, a length of string, a flint stick, and half a dozen homemade fish hooks.

Hannah's mother rolled up their thin quilts and tied the ends of the quilts with string. Then she fashioned shoulder straps from scrap linen Talitha had brought them from the big house.

After that, Hannah's mother removed a piece of ash cake and a chunk of cornbread from the hearth. She had been up late cooking the night before.

Hannah's mother placed the food in a small cloth sack along with some salt, herbs, and spices. Meanwhile, Hannah's father gathered up everyone's spare clothing and placed it in the gunny sack.

The whole process took less than ten minutes. When everything was packed, Hannah's father shouldered the bed rolls and picked up the gunny sack. Then the family quietly stepped outside and slipped away from the plantation under the cover of darkness.

Cloud cover obscured the moon as they fled. The night sky remained overcast for the first few miles of their journey. Then the clouds dissipated and the moon illuminated the nightscape.

The fugitive slave family stayed in the shadows along the edge of the dirt road as they headed north, always on the lookout for patrollers. Hannah's father continually looked over his shoulder for them.

The family was four miles north of the plantation when night riders suddenly loomed in the road up ahead. Patrollers on horseback—three of them. Each rider carried a pine torch.

Hannah's father quickly led the family off the road and into the woods. About fifty feet into the woods, he motioned for everyone to lie on the ground. He raised his left hand and placed his index finger against his lips. They could see the torches through the breaks in the trees as the riders neared. Hannah felt her blood pulsating in her ears, just like the night before when Talitha informed them that the massa's cousin planned to take her mother away.

They waited in silence as the patrollers passed by. When the torches could no longer be seen, Hannah's father crept back to the road. When he was sure the danger had passed, he motioned to the family and they resumed their journey north.

The four of them walked all night. When the first tint of pink appeared on the horizon the following morning, they were nine miles away from the plantation.

Hannah's father led the family off the road and into a thick stand of pines. About a hundred yards in from the road they came to a felled pine tree. Its upturned roots protruded skyward. Hannah's father had discovered the blowdown when he scouted the area a few weeks before. It was the farthest north he had been.

Hannah's mother untied the quilts and spread them out on the ground behind the upturned roots that shielded them from view. Then they ate ash cake. After that, the four of them laid down on the quilts and fell asleep as the sun began to edge up over the horizon.

The family remained in the stand of pines until nightfall. Then they headed back to the dirt road and continued north under the cover of darkness. They walked in moon shadows along the edge of the road as they had the night before.

The four of them had only been on the road for ten minutes when they saw torches up ahead. A slave patrol. Once again, the family abandoned the road and hid in the woods until the patrollers passed by on horseback.

Two hours later, the road cut to the west. Hannah's father looked up at the North Star, then turned off the road. He led his family northward across a section of farmland. From that point on, they would rely on the North Star to guide them on their quest for freedom.

The farmland eventually gave way to swampland. The fugitive slave family settled down on an island in the middle of the swamp just before sunup. The ash cake was gone. They ate the last of the cornbread and then they slept.

The family followed the same pattern in the days that followed, traveling only at night and sleeping during the day. Their provisions were nearly depleted. Hannah's father foraged for food. He harvested wild mushrooms and dug edible roots and wild potatoes. He cut strips of rawhide and made snares in an attempt to harvest rabbits, but he had better luck fishing.

Bait was plentiful. There were plenty of earthworms underneath rotted logs. Using a simple handline—a length of string, a rock weight, and a handmade hook—he caught catfish, sunfish, and bluegills in secluded ponds and slow-moving streams. Hannah's mother cooked the fish in the small cast iron skillet over sheltered campfires.

Just before dawn on their sixth day on the run, the family settled down in a thick ravine. The ravine's dense undergrowth—holly trees and briers—concealed their position. In the distance was a farmhouse. They could see the amber glow of a kerosene lamp through the farmhouse's back window.

*****

Edgar Barnette stepped into the tavern for an early supper that evening. A repulsive, unkempt man with a bulbous nose and long greasy hair, he ate alone. Someone had left a *Gazette* on the bar, and he grabbed it on the way over to his usual table. The man never paid for the *Gazette*.

As he waited for his supper and spirits, Edgar Barnette eagerly flipped through the pages of the *Gazette* to find what he was searching for: *fugitive slave notices*. When he came across a notice for an entire family of runaways, his face creased in an evil grin.

Two adults and two children. In his profession he wouldn't come across a better opportunity. Slave catchers spent most of their time chasing down male runaway slaves. Finding and capturing a runaway slave to return for a reward wasn't always an easy task. But an entire family was a different matter altogether. A family couldn't travel as fast as a lone man. The young ones would slow the adults down. This was a rare opportunity. And potentially a highly profitable one. The reward was one hundred fifty dollars—fifty dollars for each adult and twenty-five dollars for each child. Edgar Barnette would set out after the fugitive slave family at first light.

*****

As was their custom, the family spent the day in hiding. Late that afternoon, Hannah's father foraged for food. He headed down the ravine toward a field. The farmhouse they had spotted the day before was just seventy yards beyond the far edge of the field. Hannah's father moved slowly and crouched down as he neared the field.

He could see the farmhouse in more detail now. It was a simple two-story home, nothing at all like the big house back on the plantation.

Behind the farmhouse were several outbuildings, a barn, and a small yard. In the yard was a clothes line. It was strung between two cherry trees. Draped over the clothes line was a quilt. It swayed slightly in the breeze.

Back on the plantation, when the overseer was out of earshot, there had been talk of people who were opposed to slavery. The anti-slavery people were referred to as abolitionists. The abolitionists were said to help runaway slaves. They provided *safe houses* for runaways.

Hannah's father had heard talk about certain signs that revealed safe houses. It had been said that signs were sometimes embedded in quilts. A house with a smoking chimney was one such sign he recalled.

Hannah's father crept closer to try to see if there was a house with a smoking chimney on the quilt. But the clothes line was in the middle of the yard, too far from the tall grass he was crouched in. He couldn't make out any patterns on the quilt from his vantage point. He was about to turn around and head back to the ravine when a middle-aged woman stepped out from the house. She was carrying a basket of laundry. The runaway slave froze as the woman walked into the yard.

The woman hummed as she made her way to the clothes line. Unlike the missus back on the plantation, this woman wore simple clothing: a pale blue cotton work dress and a white bonnet. A dark woolen shawl was draped across her shoulders.

The runaway watched from his hiding place as she hung laundry on the clothes line. Then she slowly turned around and spotted him. Their eyes locked. The runaway tensed. He was about to make a run for the ravine when a slow smile creased the woman's face. The runaway remained in his position in the tall grass.

The woman discretely looked around, then slowly walked over to him. She looked into his eyes when she approached him. "It is not safe yet," she whispered. "Come back tonight when the moon is over the tree line. Come to the back door and knock three times."

The woman gestured to an outbuilding about fifty yards distant in the tall grass. "You can stay there for now. But stay hidden until nightfall."

The runaway sensed a kindness in the woman's hazel eyes. "Much obliged, ma'am," he whispered.

"Are there others?" she asked.

"Yes'm. My wife and two chillen."

"Okay. You best go now."

*****

Edgar Barnette woke before dawn. He stuffed provisions into a gunny sack. Then he tucked two pistols in his belt, grabbed his rifle, and headed out to the barn to saddle his horse and gather the bloodhounds.

Barnette arrived at the plantation just after sunup. The overseer brought him to the one-room cabin the fugitive slave family had occupied. There he found a scrap of clothing that had been left behind. Barnette let the hounds sniff it, and then he unleashed them.

The hounds wasted no time. The recent overcast, cool weather was in their favor. Scent lasted longer in cool weather. The bloodhounds had no trouble picking up the runaway slave family's trail.

Several hours later, the hounds reached the blowdown where the family had camped their first night on the run. That afternoon, the hounds sniffed around the perimeter of a swamp. They howled when they detected scent on a trail just north of the swamp.

*****

The moon was clearly visible above the tree line. Hannah's father knocked three times on the back door of the farmhouse. Hannah, her mother, and Edson were crouched in the tall grass beyond the backyard. They watched as a middle-aged woman opened the door. There was a man beside her, the woman's husband, they guessed. The man and woman talked with Hannah's father for a few moments. Then Hannah's father turned around and waved. Hannah, her mother, and Edson tentatively stepped out from the tall grass and walked toward the house.

It turned out the couple that owned the house were Quakers. Their names were William and Grace, and they were opposed to slavery.

Once the family was inside the house, William led them down a staircase to the cellar. When they got there, William lit a kerosene lamp. "It's safer down here," he said, "away from prying eyes. Upstairs, someone walking by on the road out front might spot you through the windows. But down here you're safe. Grace will bring you some food."

"This is most kind of you, suh," Hannah's mother told the man. "Most kind."

William smiled. "It's the least we can do after all that you folks have endured. Now, there's something important you need to be aware of. One never knows when patrollers or slave catchers might stop by and snoop around. If there's danger, I will bang on the floor above three times. That is your signal to go down there." William pointed to a pile of corn husks on the cellar floor. He brushed them away to reveal a trap door. William lifted the trap door which covered a wide hole in the cellar floor. "If there is trouble, go down there and close the door behind you. Don't come out until I give you the okay."

"Yes, suh." Hannah's parents nodded. Then Grace came down the stairs. She was carrying a tray of food. She set the tray down on an upturned apple crate. On the tray was a plate of sliced ham, hot biscuits, and four mugs of cider. "You must be famished," she said. "Please, eat."

"Thank you, ma'am. This is most kind of you. Most kind, indeed."

As the family ate, William talked of a plan. "I'm traveling to Wheeling on December 24th—the day after tomorrow. I'll smuggle you

126

folks there in the back of my wagon. When we reach Wheeling, I'll bring you to the bank of the Ohio River. We need to get you across the river— to the Ohio side. Ohio is a free state. An acquaintance of mine lives in a house across the river. I'll signal him at nightfall, and he'll come across the river in his boat to pick you up. He will put you up for the night and bring you to the next depot."

"Depot?"

"Safe house," William clarified. "A safe house along the *underground railroad*. There are a number of them on the route to Canada. Your destination is Canada, is it not?"

Hannah's father nodded.

"This is good," William acknowledged. "Ohio is a free state as I said, but that just means that people can't own slaves in the state; there's still danger. Not everyone in Ohio is anti-slavery. Ohio has its share of slave catchers and bounty hunters, too. Because of the Fugitive Slave Act, runaway slaves can be captured in Ohio and returned to the South."

Chapter 22

December 24, 1858

William woke the family a half hour before dawn. The four runaways gathered their few belongings and followed him up the stairs and out the back door. He led them to the barn.

Once inside the barn, he lit a kerosene lantern. In the amber light the family saw a team of horses hitched to a wagon. In the bottom of the wagon were several quilts over a bed of hay. Nestled in the right corner of the wagon was a jug of cider and a sack of food that Grace had prepared for their journey. Beside the wagon was a large pile of holly that William had harvested in the ravine the day before.

The family climbed into the wagon, and William instructed them to lie down. Once the four of them were lying prone on the wagon floor, William covered them with a burlap tarp. Then he piled holly on top of the tarp. Soon, the wagon was filled with holly, and there was no sign of the tarp. To passersby, it would it appear that the wagon carried only a load of holly.

William opened the barn door. Then he climbed up onto the wagon's buckboard and grabbed the reins. "Giddyup!"

*****

Edgar Barnette was pleased with the bloodhounds' performance. His hounds were among the best in the county. They had covered a lot of ground during the short period of time they had pursued the runaways, and the hounds were still hot on their trail. They neared a ravine just past noon.

The hounds howled when they located the area where the fugitive slave family had hid. From there, the hounds headed down the ravine toward a field. Barnette's face creased in an evil grin when he saw the farmhouse just beyond the edge of the field.

*****

The fugitive slave family spent the day nestled under the protective blanket of holly as the wagon headed north. The morning passed without event. But late that afternoon, as they neared the outskirts of Wheeling, the wagon suddenly slowed. William whispered, "Be still. Don't say a word."

A hundred yards up the road, a half dozen patrollers were conversing on horseback. They stopped talking and stared at William. William tipped his hat and pulled the wagon off the road and onto a narrow tote road to the right. The tote road meandered through a pine grove. "Giddyup!"

William pushed the horses to their limit as soon as the patrollers were out of sight. Five minutes later, he pulled back on the reins and the wagon came to an abrupt stop. He still sensed danger. William listened…and heard men on horseback approaching. The patrollers were closing in on them. It was a moment of truth. "We need to depart here, my friends," he whispered. "Hide in the woods and head north after nightfall. The river is only a few miles north of here. God be with you."

The fugitive slave family scrambled out of the wagon and ran into the thick pinewood forest.

"Giddyup!"

William continued down the tote road, pushing the horses to their limit once again. The patrollers caught up with him a mile later. They didn't believe William when he told them he was only carrying a load of holly. Two of the patrollers jumped up onto the wagon and stomped through the holly. They jabbed at the holly with their sabers, but the only thing they struck was the wagon's wooden floor.

The runaways could hear the patrollers' voices from their hiding place in the woods. They remained silent. Nobody moved an inch. Minutes ticked by like hours as they lay there on the forest floor.

The patrollers moved on, eventually, but the family waited for the sun to go down before making their next move. When the North Star was visible in the night sky, the family followed it north—toward the Ohio River.

It took them just under two hours to find the riverbank. Moonlight shimmered on the Ohio River's slow-moving water. The river was much wider than they had anticipated. Without William there to signal his contact on the other side, the family was at a loss. The four of them huddled under a stand of trees along the riverbank and contemplated their situation. The temperature had dropped significantly since sundown; Hannah and Edson shivered in their thin, tattered coats.

The family waited along the riverbank for some time in hope that word of their arrival had somehow reached William's contact on the Ohio side. But there was no sign of anyone.

Across the river, high up on a bluff, stood a grand Federal-style home. Lantern light emanated from one of its second floor windows. Hannah's parents talked in hushed voices. Was a lantern in an upper level window a sign that the home was a *safe house*? Neither of Hannah's parents recalled mention of it during conversation back in the fields... They could only hope that the lantern *was* a sign.

"I'm going to swim across the river," Hannah's father announced.

Hannah's mother, Clarissa, gasped. "You can't. The water is freezing. You'll perish. There must be another way."

"It's our only choice. I'll be fine. Chances are there's a boat along the riverbank below the bluff. I'll row back and bring you all across."

"What if there *isn't* a boat?"

"I'll go up to the house and knock on the door." Hannah's father hugged his children and kissed his wife. Then he plunged into the icy waters of the Ohio River and started for the opposite bank. Hannah, her mother, and Edson were spellbound as they watched him attempt to make his way across the river. Cloud cover obscured the moon when he was a hundred yards out. They lost sight of him.

Exhaustion set in quickly. Hannah's father's body was going numb in the frigid water, but he forged on with steadfast determination, intent on reaching the opposite shoreline. When he finally reached the Ohio shoreline, he stumbled out of the water. The man was shaking. He was suffering from hypothermia.

There was a rowboat on the shoreline below the bluff, but he knew he'd never make it back across the river in his condition. Rowing across the river was not an option. His clothing was stiffening with ice. The runaway needed shelter and warmth if he was to survive the night.

A set of wooden stairs lead up the bluff. Hannah's father struggled up the stairs. Then he made his way across a small field toward the house. Above the home's front steps was a portico supported by two fluted columns adorned with pine garlands.

He struggled up the front walk and up the stairs. Knocking on the door was almost beyond his abilities.

A tall, impeccably dressed man came to the door. He was clad in a charcoal frock coat and dark woolen trousers. Underneath the frock coat he wore a white high-collar dress shirt and a black silk puff tie.

The man's eyebrows lifted when he saw the runaway slave standing on the front stoop. "Come in! Come in!" he beckoned.

A wave of warmth washed over Hannah's father as he stepped into the front foyer. "Let's get you in front of the hearth, pronto," the tall man said. "This way."

Hannah's father followed the man down a wide hallway and then into a large drawing room where a fire blazed in an expansive brick hearth. Across the room, two children—a boy and girl—were sitting on the floor in front of a Christmas tree. They appeared to be the same ages as his children. Both of them looked up at the runaway slave.

"Abigail, get your mother," the tall man said. "Tell her to bring blankets. Joshua, fetch a bottle of brandy."

The children sensed the urgency. They wasted no time.

Hannah's father stood in front of the hearth, cherishing the heat.

"You need to get out of those clothes," the man said.

Just then, the man's wife, a middle-aged woman, rushed into the room with a pile of folded blankets. She, too, was dressed in formal attire—a wool walking skirt and a calico blouse. Fastened to her collar was a cameo brooch. "Heavens!" she said, handing the blankets to her husband. "I'll go boil water. We need to get this poor man into a hot bath right away!"

"I've got no time for a bath, ma'am," the runaway said through chattering teeth. "My family is waiting for me."

"Where is your family?"

"On the riverbank—on the Virginia side of the river."

The tall man nodded. "I'll get you some dry clothes. Then we'll go get your family."

Fifteen minutes later, they shoved off in the rowboat. Hannah's father sat in the bow, his teeth still chattering. The tall man—he introduced himself as Charles—rowed. A southwest wind impeded his efforts, but Charles was a capable rower and made good progress.

Hannah's father's eyes were intent on the Virginia shoreline. When they were halfway across the river, he noticed the glow of a campfire in the location where his family waited. A chill ran up his spine. His wife knew better than to make a fire in such an exposed location. Fires could reveal a runaway's position to slave catchers. Something was terribly wrong.

*****

134

After what seemed an eternity, the rowboat neared the Virginia shoreline. Four people loomed into view in the glowing light of a campfire: Hannah, her mother, Edson...and a repulsive man with long, greasy unkempt hair. In the man's hand was a pistol. He was holding the family at gunpoint.

The woman at the farmhouse hadn't disclosed the runaway slave family's whereabouts to Edgar Barnette that afternoon when he knocked on her door, the hounds yelping behind him. In fact, she told him she didn't know anything about any runaway slaves. But Barnette knew she wasn't telling the truth. He wasn't new to the business.

The hounds picked up a scent trail by the farmhouse's back door. From there, the hounds led Barnette to the barn, and he quickly noted the fresh wagon tracks leading away from the barn. Barnette knew right away where the wagon was headed.

Edgar Barnette snickered as the rowboat's bow touched the shoreline. "Well, well, well," he said, directing his attention to Charles. "Thanks for returning that runaway. Now I'll receive the full reward."

Hannah's father contemplated how he could overpower the gruesome slave catcher. But he was in grave shape from his perilous swim across the river. His teeth still chattered and he was chilled to the bone.

Charles stepped out of the boat and pulled it up on shore. Then Hannah's father disembarked. The two of them slowly approached the campfire. "You're expecting a reward you say?" Charles asked the slave catcher.

Edgar Barnette snickered again, his rotted teeth visible in the firelight. "That's right. Fifty dollars for each adult. Twenty-five dollars per child." He trained the pistol on Hannah's father now.

Charles looked Edgar Barnette in the eye. Then he said, "I have a better proposition for you."

Barnette spit tobacco juice into the fire and laughed. "I doubt it."

"Don't be so sure. I'll give you three hundred dollars—twice what you'd make if you return this family to the plantation."

Charles removed a billfold from his inner coat pocket. Edgar Barnette's eyes grew wide at the sight of it. Charles removed a hundred dollars from the billfold and waved it in front of Barnette. "I've got a hundred dollars on me. I'll give it to you now and go back across the river and return with the rest of the money so you can be on your way. I won't be long."

"Go right ahead," the slave catcher sneered. "These four stay with me until you return."

Charles shook his head. "No. They come with me. They're freezing. They've been through enough."

"No deal." Barnette spat in the fire again. He pointed his pistol at Charles now.

Charles furrowed his brow. "Tell you what. Have you had dinner yet?"

Barnette shook his head. There had been no time for dinner. He was famished.

"I'll sweeten the deal," Charles said. "My wife cooked a wonderful holiday meal: turkey, stuffing, mashed potatoes, sweet potatoes, collard greens, and biscuits. Oh, and plum pudding for desert."

Barnette salivated.

"You let me bring this family across the river, and I'll return with the other two hundred dollars—and a meal you won't soon forget. Heck, I'll even include some ale."

Barnette pondered the offer for a few moments. Then he said, "It's against my better judgment. But okay. I'll trust you. I'll take that hundred dollars now. And I'll be waiting right here for the rest of the money."

Charles handed Barnette the cash. "A wise decision."

Edgar Barnette watched as the four runaways hopped into the boat with their meager possessions. After they were settled in the boat, Charles pushed off and hopped in. He manned the oars and rowed toward the Ohio side of the river with all of his might. Soon the campfire on the riverbank was just a spark.

When the bow of the rowboat eventually touched the Ohio shoreline, Charles hopped out and pulled the boat onshore. The family disembarked and followed him up a set of wooden stairs and then across a field to the house.

Charles's wife—Bessie—greeted them at the front door. "Welcome! Come in, come in," she said. "Let's get you all warmed up!"

Bessie gently ushered the family inside and led them into the drawing room. The warmth emanating from the roaring fire in the hearth was a welcome reprieve. Hannah's family gathered around the hearth, and Bessie headed off to the kitchen to gather food and boil water for tea. Then Charles addressed the family. "You're safe here. I've got an errand to run. See you folks in a bit."

The boy and the girl were still sitting in front of the Christmas tree. Spread out on the floor in front of them were sheets of paper, a strip of ribbon, a pencil, a pair of scissors, and a wooden ruler. They glanced up at Hannah and Edson. Then the girl got up and walked over to Hannah. "Would you like to help us decorate the Christmas tree?" she asked.

Hannah nodded. She followed the girl over to the Christmas tree, and they sat on the floor next to each other. Edson followed suit a few minutes later and sat next to the boy.

They learned the girl's name was Abigail, and the boy's name was Joshua.

"What are you making?" Hannah asked.

"Ornaments," Abigail replied. "Angel ornaments. Have you made them before?"

Hannah shook her head. "No." Slaves didn't have Christmas trees in their cabins back on the plantation.

"They're easy to make," Abigail stated. "I'll show you. We make a dozen angel ornaments each Christmas Eve—one for each of the twelve days of Christmas."

Abigail picked up the ruler and placed it along the top edge of a piece of paper. Then she made small marks with a pencil every half inch. After that she picked up the ruler again, and using it as a guide, she folded the paper at the first half-inch mark. At the next half-inch mark, she folded the paper in the opposite direction. She repeated the process until there was a fold at each mark and the paper took on an accordion-like shape.

Abigail then compressed the paper by pressing the two outer edges together. Once the paper was compressed, she tied a ribbon about a third of the way down from the top of the paper. Next, she spread the portion of the paper below the ribbon like a fan. She did the same with the smaller portion above the ribbon, too. Then she picked up a pair of scissors and trimmed the smaller section at the top into a circular shape. After that, she cut a notch at the top and divided the top section into two wings.

Abigail handed the angel-shaped ornament to Edson. "You can place this on the tree if you like." Edson grinned.

The four of them soon fell into a comfortable rhythm. Joshua and Edson marked papers and folded them. Abigail and Hannah compressed the papers and fashioned each piece of paper into an angel ornament, using scissors and ribbon.

Bessie returned with a tray containing a steaming pot of tea and a half dozen porcelain cups. She set the tray on a rosewood end table and poured hot tea into the cups. She then handed a cup to each of Hannah's parents. They thanked the woman for her kindness as she headed back to the kitchen for food.

*****

Charles was absent for some time. He returned shortly before midnight accompanied by another man. The two of them stepped into the drawing room. The children were hanging handcrafted angel ornaments on the Christmas tree, and the adults were sitting down sipping tea and talking in front of the hearth.

Hannah's parents were alarmed when they looked up and saw the man with Charles. He was dressed altogether differently than Charles. This fellow wore overalls and an old wool coat. But Charles's smile assured them that all was well. "You needn't worry about that slave catcher," he told them. "Clem and I gave that scoundrel quite a scare."

Clem nodded. "That's right," he confided. "That slave catcher hightailed it after we exchanged words, and he saw he was outgunned. I don't expect we'll be seeing the likes of him around here ever again."

Just then, there was a knock at the door. Charles left the room to answer it. He returned a few minutes later accompanied by Clem's wife and daughter. Each of them held a bundle of used clothing and blankets. Clem's daughter joined the children by the Christmas tree, while his wife handed the clothing and blankets to Hannah's parents. "We heard about your plight," she said. "These should help."

Tears welled in Hannah's mother's eyes as she accepted the gifts. "Thank you. Thank you so much."

"I wish we could give you more."

Just then, Charles reached into his inner jacket pocket. He removed his billfold and extracted a hundred dollars. "It turns out that slave catcher didn't take my money after all," he said with a wry grin. "This should help you reach your destination." He handed the money to Hannah's father.

Hannah's father stared at the money. Tears welled in his eyes now, too. He was too choked up to speak. Charles patted him on the back and said, "Let's have some wassail."

The children sang carols in front of the Christmas tree while the adults drank wassail and chatted. Eventually, the fire in the hearth diminished and Clem and his wife and daughter left. Hannah's family was then led upstairs to the guest bedroom. That night, for the first time in their lives, the four of them slept in real beds—feather beds.

*****

The family celebrated Christmas in Canada the following year. And they would celebrate many more Christmases in the years ahead, but none of them would be quite like the Christmas of 1858.

Chapter 23

"That was quite a story," I remarked. As with my grandmother's tale earlier that afternoon, I had become totally absorbed in Eleanor's story.

Eleanor looked at me. "My great grandchildren ask me to tell them the story each Christmas."

I glanced over at the Christmas tree and took in the angel ornaments. My interest wasn't lost on Eleanor. She got up and slowly made her way over to the tree. Then she gently removed an angel ornament from one of the lower branches. She handed it to me. "For your Christmas Tin," she said.

I smiled. "Thank you, Eleanor. This will be a most welcome addition."

My grandmother looked at her watch and announced that it was time for us to leave. We donned our coats and Eleanor walked us to the front door.

After expressing our thanks to Eleanor, we made our way outside to the SUV. It was dark out. I looked up at the North Star and thought about Hannah and her family.

*****

We ate dinner—steak, roasted potatoes, brussel sprouts, and salad—in my grandparents' living room. The television was on, and we watched the evening news as we dined. The weather forecast caught my attention.

"Snow is headed our way," the weatherman announced. "It should start by mid-morning tomorrow and will intensify throughout the day. Accumulations of eight to ten inches are expected. And there will be more snow on Sunday. Heavy, wind-driven snow..."

"I suppose I should plan to leave tomorrow," I informed my grandparents.

My grandfather nodded. "An early start would be wise."

Chapter 24

When I stepped into the kitchen the following morning, a box lunch was on the counter. Beside it was a loaf of pumpkin bread wrapped in tinfoil. My grandmother was sitting at the kitchen table filling a thermos with coffee. She smiled when she saw me. Then she handed me the thermos. "To keep you awake on the ride home," she said. "I packed a lunch and the pumpkin bread on the counter is for you, too. Try not to eat all of it on the way home. Mariana and Paul might enjoy some, too," she joked.

"I'll try to remember," I smiled. "Thanks, Grandma. You are the best."

"You are most welcome, sweetheart."

"Is Grandpa home?"

"No. He's over at Bronson's place. Your grandfather is helping Bronson repair a tractor."

"Well, I should be pushing off," I said. We hugged.

"Give Mariana and Paul my best."

"Will do, Grandma. Thanks for everything. See you next week."

"Bye, sweetheart. Drive safely."

"I will."

*****

My mind drifted during the drive home. I reflected on my grandmother's story. I thought about Eleanor's story, too. Their stories had provided a pleasant distraction from my financial worries. A welcome reprieve. The stories also gave me cause to look at my current financial situation from a different perspective.

Compared to the hardships endured by the people in the stories, my situation didn't seem quite so dire. I had options that the people in the stories didn't have. I could sell my SUV. I could sell our home if it came down to it. And there was the opportunity to collect unemployment. The people in the stories didn't have any safety nets—but they persevered nonetheless. And maybe I would, too, I began to think.

*****

When I turned onto Route 7 and continued south, my thoughts transitioned to the upcoming lunch meeting with Steve Harrington, Jake Templeton, and Ike Coldwell. I wondered again about the nature of the meeting. My hunch was that the three of them were looking to self-manage their buildings and were likely looking for some friendly advice.

Beldon is a small town. Beyond Central New England Real Estate Group, there are no nearby property management firms that the investors could reach out to. I looked forward to providing any advice I could. They had always been good to me. I started to compile a mental list of reputable local contractors I could refer them to, guys like Bud Clements who would be there for them.

Wendy texted me as I pulled into a gas station shortly before the state line. She provided that the name of the restaurant that Gisueppi

Moretti selected for dinner Monday evening: Agostina's—a new Italian restaurant in downtown Beldon. Gisueppi would be there at seven o'clock. I looked forward to catching up with the man and would do my best to help him out, too, if I could.

.

*****

Mariana was waiting for me when I got home. She wrapped her arms around me and pulled me into an embrace. We kissed. Then she said, "Welcome home... We have a little problem."

"Oh?"

"The basement is flooded."

I winced. Visions of water emanating from our old boiler loomed to the forefront of my thoughts. I hoped the boiler wasn't shot. A new boiler would deplete our remaining savings.

I walked down the stairs to the basement expecting the worst. The basement floor was under three inches of water, but thankfully the concrete slab under the boiler was dry. The boiler was okay.

I breathed a sigh of relief. Then I looked around and quickly determined the source of the water: a leak in a cold water pipe. Water was emanating from a small hole in the pipe. I turned the pipe's shutoff valve to the off position. Then I went out to the workshop in the garage and cut a patch from an old inner tube, grabbed a few hose clamps and a screwdriver from my toolbox, and headed back to the basement.

It took less than five minutes to patch the pipe, but it was only a temporary fix. The next step was to call the plumber.

147

Bud Clements arrived twenty minutes after I called him. "Hey, Jesse!" Bud boomed. "Good to see you!"

"Likewise, Bud. Thanks for coming out so quickly."

"No problem."

Bud made quick work of cutting out the section of rotted pipe. We chatted as he soldered in a new section of copper pipe. "Did you hear what happened over at Beldon Gardens?" he asked.

"No," I replied. "Been out of town."

"The boiler went down last week. It was only five years old. The problem was likely just a minor maintenance issue involving the burner motor, perhaps just a clogged nozzle—a quick fix. Central New England Real Estate Group called in a contractor they do business with in Boston. The guy ended up replacing the entire boiler. The owner of Beldon Gardens, Ike Coldwell, was livid about the situation."

"That's unfortunate." Ike had a right to be angry. The meeting with him, Steve, and Jake on Monday would be interesting to say the least.

Chapter 25

Monday, December 21

I pulled into the lot in front of Nick's Diner just before noon. A string of Christmas lights framed the diner's front door, and fogged window glass bespoke the warmth inside the diner. Upon entering the establishment, I was greeted by a wave of cacophony: the clank of plates and silverware, gossip, and carols emanating from table-top jukeboxes. The diner had changed very little over the years. It was my kind of place.

Steve, Jake, and Ike were already seated at a booth along the far wall. The three of them stood up as I approached the booth. We shook hands and exchanged pleasantries for a few minutes. Then we sat down.

"Jesse, great to see you," Steve said. "Thanks for meeting with us."

"My pleasure, Steve. Great to see all of you as well."

"The family doing well?" Steve inquired.

"They are," I replied. "They're looking forward to the holidays. We're going to spend Christmas at my grandparents' farm in Vermont. I was just up there."

"Yes, Wendy informed us. Vermont is a great place to visit this time of year."

The waitress came over just then with a pot of coffee and a small pitcher of cream. She was wearing a Santa hat. She placed the pitcher of cream on the table and filled our mugs with coffee before taking our order. The four of us opted for the lunch special.

After the waitress left, Steve said, "Jesse, you're probably wondering about the nature of this get together."

I took a sip of coffee. "Yes."

"Well, we'll get right to it. You may have heard that the transition with Central New England Real Estate Group has been rocky."

I nodded.

"We won't waste your time delving into the details. I'm guessing you have probably heard about some of the problems we've experienced since Central New England Real Estate Group assumed the management of our properties. Suffice it to say, we are not happy with the new management firm."

"Indeed," Ike put in.

"That's right," Jake agreed. "To put it lightly."

"I'm sorry to hear that," I said. "I wouldn't have expected it."

"It's been enlightening," Steve remarked.

"Eye-opening," Jake put in.

Ike nodded in agreement. "Ditto."

"Jesse, as you know, our management contracts expire on December 31st," Steve continued. "We are *not* interested in renewing our management contracts with Central New England Real Estate Group. We have seen enough."

"Are you planning to self-mange?" I asked.

Steve grinned. "No—we'd like *you* to manage our properties."

I was awestruck. I hadn't anticipated this at all. My assumption had been that the three of them would opt to self-manage their buildings, and that they were just looking for some friendly advice. When the shock wore off, I said, "Gentleman, I'm flattered. Could you give me a day or two to run some numbers and do some research?"

"How about if we meet here again in two days—the same time on Wednesday?" Steve suggested. "Would that give you enough time?"

"You bet," I said. "I look forward to it."

"As do we, Jesse."

*****

My mind was reeling on the drive home. I had a lot of thinking to do. As soon as I got home, I brought the laptop to the kitchen table. I quickly tabulated the potential revenue from management fees for the three investor-owned properties. Then I subtracted some hypothetical expenses—office rent, utilities, insurance, fiduciary bond. At first glance, it appeared that the net income would be significantly less than my former salary, but the idea of working for myself held appeal.

It was exciting to think about the possibility of self-employment, but as I researched pricing for commercial insurance policies and office space that afternoon, it became evident that making a living from three property management contracts alone would not be possible in my case. Still, I tried to remain hopeful.

Before I knew it, it was six-thirty. I had a half hour to get to Agostina's.

*****

I liked Agostina's as soon as I entered the establishment. The walls in the vestibule were adorned with prints of Venice and the Toscano Valley; an Italian love song softly emanated from the ceiling speakers. A plaque above the reception desk read *Buon Natale—Merry Christmas.*

The ambiance was warm and friendly, if not romantic. It was a place Mariana would no doubt like. I'd have to bring her sometime.

"You must be Jesse Maclean," the young woman behind the reception desk announced.

"I am."

"Right this way, please."

The hostess led me down a small hallway to the dining area. There were a dozen tables in the center of the room. All of them were covered with red and white checkered tablecloths. Atop each table was a green wine bottle with a white candle. A series of booths lined the left wall, and along the right wall was a long counter. Behind the counter was an open kitchen where a chef was sautéing vegetables in a cast iron skillet.

Gisueppi was seated at a table in the middle of the room. On the table in front of him was an assortment of appetizers—bruschetta, basil pesto bread, stromboli bites, and melon balls wrapped in prosciutto. Gisueppi smiled and stood up when he saw me. I made my way over to him, and we shook hands. For a moment there, I thought the man might hug me.

"Jesse, so good you are here. So good to see you again, my friend."

I smiled. "Likewise, Gisueppi. I've been looking forward to it."

"Please, sit down. We'll get caught up. I want to tell you about my trip to Italy."

Gisueppi gestured to the tray of appetizers on the table as we sat down across from each other. "Just a little something to tide us over until the main course."

I opted for a slice of basil pesto bread. It was delicious. As we snacked on appetizers, Gisueppi asked about my family. Then he told me about his trip to Italy. He mentioned a little bit about his childhood in Italy, too. Gisueppi talked of playing soccer and bocce ball with his friends during his youth. He described festive family gatherings and Sunday meals at his grandparents' home. He also talked about his early days in America.

When I inquired about his family, Gisueppi said, "My daughter, Marietta, she is a marketing executive. Marietta and her husband live in California. And my son, Gastone, is a surgeon. He and his family live in New York City. I plan to spend Christmas with them. Have you been to New York City during the holidays?"

I shook my head. "No, but I've always wanted to."

"Wonderful place. You and your wife must go there some time."

The waitress came to our table to take our order just then. I hadn't perused the menu yet, so I looked it over while Gisueppi ordered. "I would like the linguine di mare," he requested.

"That sounds interesting. What is it?"

Gisueppi grinned. "Linguine and seafood—lobster, shrimp, clams, and mussels."

"I'll take the same," I informed the waitress.

"An excellent choice," Gisueppi remarked. "You will not be disappointed. Their pasta is homemade."

Dinner surpassed my expectations. The seafood must have been trucked straight from the docks that morning. It was phenomenal. After dinner, we ordered espresso. The tiramisu on the dessert menu was tempting, but I had no room left for dessert.

We hadn't discussed business at all. The subject of real estate had not come up, and I assumed the dinner was intended as a social visit—which was fine by me. I enjoyed Gisueppi's company, and the food was outstanding.

When Gisueppi's espresso cup was almost empty, he cleared his throat and looked at me. "Jesse, there is something I'd like to discuss with you."

"You have my attention."

"My buildings…are a bit too much for me to handle by myself these days. I don't want to retire yet, though. I want to stay involved in the business. I enjoy the business, but it has been somewhat difficult for me lately. My wife and I like to travel. We plan to spend more time in Italy next year. It is hard to get away now, harder than in the past.

"I'm in need of a partner, Jesse. Someone who could take care of things while I am away. Someone who could, perhaps, manage the operations of some of the larger properties, and take over the business one day. My kids—they are not interested in the business. They are busy with their own lives.

"Jesse, I want to ask if you may be interested in a partnership. I don't have the details worked out yet, but I have a feeling we could work something out."

For the second time that day, I was awestruck. "Gisueppi, would you care for another espresso?"

Gisueppi grinned. "Yes. I happen to like espresso very much."

Chapter 26

Steve, Jake, and Ike were seated at the same booth when I stepped into Nick's Diner at noon on Wednesday. Like two days before, all three of them stood up as I made my way over and we shook hands. We exchanged pleasantries for a few minutes and discussed holiday plans. Then the waitress came over and took our lunch orders. This time she was wearing a green elf hat. When she left, Steve said, "Jesse, the floor is yours."

"Thanks, Steve." I reached into my briefcase and removed three envelopes. One for each of them. I distributed the envelopes. "Gentlemen," I began. "I want to thank you for your trust and confidence in me. I would welcome the opportunity to assume the management of your properties. Inside your envelope, you'll find a property management proposal and a management contract. You'll also find a certificate of insurance."

Each of them opened their envelope and perused the documents. As they looked everything over, I informed them of my new partnership with Gisueppi and told them I'd be working out of an office in one of Gisueppi's downtown buildings.

"It appears you have been quite busy the past few days," Steve commented. "This is impressive, Jesse."

Jake and Ike nodded in agreement as they studied their documents.

"I *have* been busy," I acknowledged. I didn't disclose that I had stayed up until four o'clock that morning working feverishly to complete the management proposals and contracts.

Steve placed his documents back in his envelope. Then he placed the envelope on the table. "It looks like you have everything well covered, Jesse," he said. "I'll look everything over in more detail this weekend, and will be in touch if I have any questions. I'll plan to drop the signed contract off at your office early next week."

"Same here," Jake announced.

"Ditto," Ike put in.

After lunch, Steve proposed a toast to a prosperous New Year for all. The four of us raised our coffee mugs in a toast. When we stepped outside afterward it was snowing—and for the first time that season, I thought about Christmas.

My cell phone rang just as I was about to pull out of the diner's parking lot. I recognized the name on Caller ID: Reginalde Kalhume. *This should be interesting.*

I picked up the cell phone and answered. "Hello, Reginalde."

"Jesse! How are you doing?!" From his tone, you'd think we were long lost friends.

"I'm doing well."

"Splendid, splendid. And your family is well?"

"Yes, they are." I was surprised he even knew that I had a family. Reginalde had never inquired about my family before. The guy had been all business previously.

"That's great. Listen, Jesse, I'd like to schedule a time for us to get together."

Get together? "Reginalde, what's the nature of this get-together, if I may ask? I'm sure I could answer any questions you have over the phone and save us both some time."

"Jesse, I'll be blunt. We'd like to rehire you."

I furrowed my brow. "*Rehire* me?"

"That's right," Reginalde confirmed. "We've now had ample time to assess the situation here. We've had time to develop a proper staffing plan."

"But, you let me go."

"That was just standard operating procedure following an acquisition. There's always an adjustment period after an acquisition as we get to know the lay of the land. It was nothing personal, just the way it's done."

"The *standard operating procedure* was never mentioned to me."

"Well, the bottom line is, we want you back, Jesse. How does your schedule look today? Could you swing by the office at three o'clock?"

"I'm not available."

"Okay. How about four o'clock? Or I could meet you later if need be, perhaps over dinner. My treat of course."

"Reginalde, I'm not interested in working for Central New England Real Estate Group. I have something else lined up."

"…Oh…I'm sorry to hear that…Is this other opportunity locked up yet? We may be able to bring you back at a higher salary."

"Sorry, Reginalde. It's a done deal. Happy holidays to you and your family."

"Uh…yeah…You too, I guess."

Chapter 27

Christmas

I was the only person in my grandparents' house for a short window of time on Christmas afternoon. Everyone else was visiting the neighboring farm. I wasn't alone though. Penny was curled up beside me on the living room floor.

I welcomed the quietude. I was still processing the recent turn of events in my life and looked forward to some quiet time to just sit back in front of the fire and reflect for a bit. For me, Christmastime has always been a time for reflection.

The sound of laughter broke my reverie. I heard the front door open and then everyone filed into the house. They hadn't been gone more than ten minutes. It was just past two o'clock. The neighbors were not home, apparently.

The six of them—my parents, grandparents, Mariana, and Paul—removed their coats, hats, and boots. Then the men retreated to the living room while my mother, grandmother, and Mariana headed into the kitchen to make a pot of tea and warm up the apple pie my mother had baked. I got up and placed a few more logs in the fireplace.

A short while later, an old Bing Crosby Christmas song emanated from the hi-fi as everyone congregated in the living room. There was a comfortable silence as we sipped hot tea and ate warm apple pie. Everyone seemed lost in thought.

My parents had claimed the two oak armchairs beside the Christmas tree.

Mariana and Paul were sitting on the braided rug in front of the fireplace. Penny was between them. I was sitting on the easy chair, and my grandparents sat next to each other on the couch. The small wooden box was on the coffee table in front of them.

My grandmother glanced at the box. Then she looked up at my grandfather. "Sweetheart," she said, "perhaps you could tell everyone the story."

My grandfather's eyebrows lifted. "What story would that be, my dear?"

My grandmother gently lifted the small wooden box from the coffee table and handed it to my grandfather. My grandfather opened its lid and peered into the box...He furrowed his brow. "I don't think anyone wants to hear that old story," he remarked. "Who's up for a game of chess?"

My grandmother shook her head. "Tell the story, sweetheart. It will do you good to tell it. And I know everyone would enjoy hearing it."

"I'd love to hear the story," Paul said.

"Same here," I chimed in.

"We all would, Dad," my father added.

My grandmother clasped my grandfather's hand. She knew this would be difficult for him. Even after all the years that had passed, talking about the war was still difficult for him. "Go on," my grandmother gently prodded. "Tell the story, sweetheart. It's a story that deserves to be told."

A few moments passed in silence. My grandfather glanced inside the box again. I expected him to back out. I think everyone did. But then he took a deep breath and set the box on the coffee table. There was a distant look in his eyes as he leaned back into the couch. "…Very well then," he said, surprising everyone.

All eyes were on my grandfather as he drifted back over the decades…

Chapter 28

December 24, 1944

Sergeant Gerald Maclean peered over the rim of the frozen foxhole as the first tints of dawn streaked the horizon. The sergeant's eyes were trained on a section of tree line that bordered the eastern edge of the field—the area where the sound had come from. The snow-laden woods of the Ardennes had been eerily quiet...until that rustling sound. It had been almost imperceptible. Sergeant Maclean wondered if he had imagined it.

Privates Danner Rigby and Cal Taylor lay huddled under a snow-dusted woolen blanket beside him. The two riflemen were still in the throes of sleep. The sergeant considered waking them but opted not to. Any unnecessary movement or sound could give away their position and alert the enemy.

The sergeant remained motionless, moving only his eyes as he scanned the tree line. The battle-scarred landscape was just becoming visible in the gray light of early dawn when he heard the sound again...A subtle footfall. Then another.

Sergeant Maclean looked down the iron sights of his Garand M1 rifle. The rifle's muzzle was pointed at the tree line. He cautiously removed the woolen glove from his right hand and pushed the safety to the off position.

The footfalls were closer now...A flicker of movement at the edge of the field caught his attention. The sergeant's heart raced as his forefinger touched the trigger. He took a deep breath, just like the instructor had preached on the rifle range during basic training back in the states...A deer cautiously emerged from the woods and stepped onto the field.

Sergeant Maclean exhaled. Venison would be a welcome addition to K-rations, but he knew better than to risk a shot and alert the enemy. The sergeant pushed the rifle's safety back to the on position.

The deer lowered its head and began to feed along the edge of the field. The sergeant glanced down at his wristwatch. He'd allow the two privates a little more rest. Lord knew they needed it.

Their orders were to fall back to the company's command post (CP) at sunrise, using a different trail, lest the enemy lie in ambush along the one they came in on.

A gust of wind swirled snow into the foxhole, underscoring the frigid conditions. Sergeant Maclean hunkered down. He pulled the collar of his field jacket up and pulled his helmet liner down over his ears. He moved his numb toes up and down inside his leather jump boots. As of late he'd been experiencing a tingling feeling in his left foot, hoped it wasn't trench foot. Many of the ill-equipped Americans had suffered from trench foot since arriving in Bastogne.

Glancing at the two privates asleep under the woolen blanket beside him, the sergeant's thoughts drifted back to the barracks the men had been billeted in just seven days before in the French town of Mourmelon-le-Grand. The members of the 101st Airborne Division had been recuperating from seventy-two days of intensive fighting in Holland.

There had been a coal heater in the barracks and hot chow. The men had been in high spirits as they enjoyed a much needed reprieve from combat. They wrote letters, slept, played craps, and relaxed for the first time in months. There was even talk of Christmas passes to Paris. But that had been before word of massive enemy troop movement in the Ardennes had reached the high command.

Hitler's plan called for an all-out German thrust through the Ardennes—a move intended to divide the American and English forces, cut their supplies, and push both the Americans and the English back to Antwerp.

The German's plan depended on the utilization of roads that cut through the Ardennes. The central Ardennes town of Bastogne, with its crucial crossroads, would be directly in the Germans' path. It didn't take the Americans long to determine the importance of Bastogne. The Americans needed to reach Bastogne first to defend the town and block access to its crossroads at all costs. The 101st Airborne Division had been selected for the job.

Sergeant Maclean and the other members of his rifle company departed Mourmelon-le-Grand on December 18th in an uncovered truck—one of 380 trucks in a convoy that transported the 101st to the Ardennes. Somebody dubbed the convoy the Red Ball Express. The name stuck.

After a frigid, bone-jarring eight-hour ride in the back of the truck, the troopers disembarked into the fog, five miles outside of Bastogne, to the sound of distant shelling. They reached Bastogne late in the afternoon of December 19th. Less than twenty-four hours later, the Germans surrounded the town.

A frigid blast of wind cut through Sergeant Maclean's field jacket. He shivered and hunkered even deeper into the frozen foxhole. In the hectic rush to reach Bastogne, winter clothing had been an afterthought. Ammunition was more crucial. It would be well into January before winter clothing would arrive. Many of the Americans lacked winter coats, galoshes, and proper gear. There was also a lack of food and a shortage of ammunition and arms. During the ride to Bastogne, one of the men in Sergeant Maclean's truck didn't even have a rifle. The only weapon the man carried was a trench knife.

The sergeant opened a K-ration and quietly ate a cold breakfast as he watched the deer feed. The deer had been feeding gracefully for five minutes when it suddenly jerked its head up and looked into the woods that bordered the eastern edge of the field. The deer remained still for a few minutes, its ears perked. Then its tail shot up and the deer bounded across the field and disappeared into the woods that bordered the western edge of the field.

Whatever had spooked the deer could not be far away. The sergeant woke the privates and gave the hand signal to be quiet. Privates Rigby and Taylor climbed out from under the snow-dusted woolen blanket and grabbed their carbines.

"Krauts?" Private Rigby whispered.

"Not sure," the sergeant replied. "Keep your eye on the tree line over there." He gestured to the eastern edge of the field.

A few minutes passed without event. Then came an eerie whistling sound…An incoming mortar. The Americans had been spotted.

The three of them huddled as deep as they could in the foxhole as the mortar struck the ground seventy yards short of their position. A German mortar team was zeroing in on their position.

They soon heard the whistling of another incoming mortar. This one was much closer. It struck the field just thirty yards to the right of the foxhole.

Sergeant Maclean quickly evaluated their options. The CP was 600 yards south of their position—600 yards of open fields and scattered hedgerows. They'd be easy targets in German gun sights. North of their position was several hundred yards of open field without so much as a slit trench for cover. Their only option was to head for the woods that bordered the western edge of the field, the thick woodland the deer had bounded into. The woods were sixty yards from the foxhole. Sixty yards of frozen field.

"Move out!" the sergeant yelled. "Follow my lead."

Sergeant Maclean leapt out of the foxhole and ran westward in a zigzag pattern. The privates were just behind him. A mortar round hit the foxhole seconds after the three of them vacated.

The Americans made a frantic dash for the woodland. Machine gun fire broke out behind them.

The sergeant was the first to reach the tree line, and the privates were not far behind. The three Americans slipped into the dense pine forest unscathed. Had the circumstances been different, they would have felt apprehensive about heading into the thick woods. Too many American lives had been lost to tree bursts from German shells.

The dense growth slowed them as they made their way into the forest. There was little space between the trees. Branches cut their faces, necks, and hands as they penetrated the forest.

A hundred yards into the forest, they discovered an old cart path. The Americans followed it. They walked single file, using only hand signals to communicate.

The sergeant took point. He walked slowly, heel-to-toe, just like his father had taught him during deer season back home. Private Rigby was behind him. Private Taylor took up the rear.

The cart path twisted and meandered through the woodland. The three of them were soon deep in the forest and could no longer see the field through the breaks in the trees. They were headed northeast now— further away from the American front line.

The cart path ended at an old stone foundation a half hour later, and the Americans found themselves in an even thicker section of woods that were nearly impenetrable. The only way to get through the area was to follow the deer trails that meandered through it.

The three Americans were ghostlike as they followed a deer trail, stopping now and then to listen for enemy activity. The sky was clear, but the trees blocked most of the sunlight, and visibility was low in this section of the Ardennes.

They had been on the deer trail for twenty minutes when it crossed a small spring. The three of them stopped to fill their canteens. Then they continued down the trail. Ten minutes later, the trail ended at the base of a knoll.

Keeping their profiles as low as possible, the Americans quietly made their way up the knoll. When they neared the top of the knoll, they got down on their hands and knees and cautiously inched their way up to the crest. Once there, they peered down at the forest on the other side of the knoll, moving only their eyes...Less than a hundred yards downhill from their position was a dugout—a fortification constructed of logs and mud. An isolated outpost. Smoke emanated from a small makeshift chimney that protruded from the dugout's dirt-covered roof.

The three Americans remained stone still as they peered down at the dugout. They had been watching the dugout for a few minutes when a soldier stepped out from the fortification. A German soldier. The enemy was smoking a cigarette. Strapped across his right shoulder was a Schmeisser machine pistol.

Behind the dugout was a well-worn trail that cut through the pines. The German soldier glanced down the trail. Then he said, *"Es gibt noch keine Spur von ihnen."* No sign of them yet.

The German tossed his cigarette on the ground and stepped on it. Then he stepped back inside the dugout.

"What now, Sarge?" whispered Private Rigby.

Just then they heard voices. German voices. On the trail behind the dugout was a column of Germans. Twelve German soldiers. They were walking single file. All of them were clad in white parkas.

Two of the Germans carried Panzerfaust anti-tank grenade launchers, another toted an MG42 machine gun. The rest carried Mauser bolt action rifles and semi-automatic Sturmgewehr 44s.

The Americans were seriously outgunned. Between them they had but two Garand M1 rifles, a Thompson submachine gun, and a .45 pistol.

The Americans cautiously backed away from the crest of the knoll. When the enemy was no longer in sight, they crept back down. After descending the knoll, the Americans headed down another deer trail—deeper into enemy territory.

This deer trail cut along a ridge which gradually gave way to a series of sparsely wooded rolling hills. Beyond the hills was a large field. The Americans could see it through the breaks in the trees as they descended the last hill.

When they neared the edge of the field, the sergeant removed his compass from the left pocket of his field coat and took a reading. He pointed to the woodland across the field. "Those woods are due south," he whispered. "If we can make it over there and continue south, we should eventually be able to make it back to the unit." The privates nodded.

The three Americans remained in the woods by the edge of the field. They surveyed the field for signs of activity. The field was pockmarked with shell holes and bomb craters. Smoke rose from an overturned jeep. Mangled artillery from both sides littered the landscape.

Ten minutes ticked by. All was quiet. The entire area seemed devoid of life.

The sergeant gave the signal and the three of them slowly stepped out from the tree line and cautiously made their way onto the field. Two hundred yards of frozen, war-torn stubble field lay between them and the woodland they needed to reach. "Let's move out," the sergeant whispered.

Sergeant Maclean crouched down to keep his profile as low as possible as he started across the field. The privates followed him. Their green field jackets contrasted sharply against the snow-covered field.

The Americans had advanced seventy yards when they heard the dreaded whistling of an incoming mortar. The men hit the ground as a mortar passed over them. It exploded when it struck the earth fifty yards beyond them. The Americans quickly got up and were about to make an all out attempt to reach the woodland across the field when a burst of machine gun fire emanated from a hedgerow west of their position—likely the same hedgerow where the German mortar team was dug in.

The Americans ducked behind a mound of earth beside a shell hole. It didn't afford much protection, but it was better than being exposed in the open.

Just then, a German tank—a Panzer—broke through the hedgerow. It headed down the field toward the Americans.

Sergeant Maclean contemplated their next move. A bomb crater twenty-five yards from their position caught his eye. It would provide more protection than the small mound of earth they were hunkered behind—if they could reach it. The bomb crater was their only hope. The Americans bolted for it, weaving around stumps and abandoned pieces of field artillery.

More machine gun fire erupted from the hedgerow. Then another mortar round struck the earth just thirty yards behind the Americans as they reached the edge of the bomb crater. There was no time to contemplate, no time to gauge the depth of the crater. The three Americans jumped into the bomb crater and plummeted eight feet before hitting ground.

When they looked up, a German soldier was pointing his Mauser rifle at them...

Chapter 29

The German stood ten feet away from them. "Drop your weapons," he commanded.

The Americans placed their carbines on the ground. The enemy instructed them to move to the opposite end of the crater. The Americans did as they were told. As they moved away from their weapons, an airplane could be heard in the distance. It was coming from the south and was headed in their direction.

The plane broke through the cloud cover and began to descend. The Americans saw it was one of theirs. A P-47 fighter. The P-47 continued to descend as it neared the field, intent on a strafing run.

The soldiers from both sides braced themselves as the P-47 approached overhead. The P-47's machine guns blared. Bullets riddled the ground on each side of the crater.

The pilot dropped bombs seconds after the plane passed overhead. Two deafening explosions followed. The earth shook.

The P-47 ascended into the clouds and headed south. The area was suddenly quiet. The Americans suspected the bombs had taken out the Panzer and possibly the mortar crew, too, but they couldn't be sure. They were unable to peer over the top edge of the bomb crater to see.

With his Mauser trained on them, the German bent down and picked up one of the American carbines with his left hand and tossed it out of the crater. Then he did the same with the other two weapons.

Sergeant Maclean studied the German. The enemy was tall and had a sturdy build, but he was older than the Americans. And there was a haggard look to him. His chin was peppered with white razor stubble; he looked old enough to be their father.

There was a .45 pistol strapped to the sergeant's belt underneath his field jacket. He would wait until nightfall to make his move.

"Comrades," the German announced. "You may sit down. We'll likely be here for a while."

The German kneeled down across from the Americans, the Mauser's muzzle still trained on them. The minutes ticked by as the Americans sat under the enemy's watchful gaze. They studied the German, took in his clothing, his winter gear.

The Germans might be losing the war, but this one was far better equipped than the Americans. He was clad in a thick grey wool overcoat and matching wool pants, and he wore insulted combat boots with metal-studded soles. Under his leather gloves were thick wool liners. His neck was shielded from the elements by a heavy woolen scarf. Even his helmet liner seemed superior.

After a while, the German reached into his coat pocket and slowly extracted a chunk of cheese and a pocketknife, his eyes never wavering from the Americans. He slowly placed the Mauser on the ground beside him within easy reach. Then he opened the pocketknife, cut a slice of cheese, and popped it in his mouth. He surprised the Americans when he cut another slice from the cheese and handed it to Private Taylor who was sitting closest to him. Private Taylor had twisted his ankle during the fall. The nineteen-year-old had been wincing in pain ever since.

Private Taylor passed on the cheese and handed it to Private Rigby. Rigby was always hungry. The sergeant had never seen anyone eat as much as that kid. Rigby took a bite of cheese and passed the rest of it to the sergeant.

The sergeant looked over at the German. "How is that you speak English so well?" he inquired.

A few moments passed in silence. Then the German said, "I was a cabbie in England before the war—the first war. The money was better over there at the time. A lot of us worked in England back then."

"How long did you work in England for?" This from Private Rigby.

"Three years."

Private Taylor winced. From the stress lines on the private's face, it was evident his pain was increasing. He constantly rubbed his right ankle now. Private Taylor's pain was not lost on the German. "I can take a look at your ankle if you like," he offered. "I was a medic during the first war."

"You fought in the Great War?" Private Rigby asked.

The German nodded. Then he motioned for Private Taylor to come over to him.

Private Taylor glanced at the sergeant. The sergeant gave him a nod. Private Taylor limped over and hesitantly sat down within arm's reach of the German.

"You wouldn't have any morphine?" Private Taylor asked.

The German shook his head no. "I wish I did." He gently removed the boot on Private Taylor's right foot. The private's ankle was severely swollen. It was twice the size of his left ankle.

The German massaged Taylor's injured ankle for several minutes Then he reached into his rucksack and extracted a small tin of pills, a tube of ointment, and a rolled up cloth bandage. He removed two pills from the tin and handed them to Private Taylor. "They'll help reduce the swelling and ease the pain."

The sergeant's .45 was within easy reach, still shielded underneath his field jacket. But it wasn't the right time to make a move for it. The P-47 had likely taken out the Panzer and the German mortar team, but that didn't change the fact that they were deep in enemy territory. The slightest noise could alert a German patrol. Nightfall was not far off He'd stick to his original plan and make his move under the cover of darkness.

Private Taylor swallowed the pills as the German applied ointment on his right ankle. After the ointment was thoroughly applied, the German began to wrap the private's ankle with the bandage.

Sergeant Maclean experienced tingling in his left foot again. He removed the boot from his left foot. Then he removed his sock. His foot was red. He massaged it in an attempt to alleviate the tingling feeling that had plagued him as of late.

The German glanced over at the sergeant as he finished wrapping the private's ankle. Then he reached into his rucksack again and extracted a small tin of talc powder. He tossed it over to the sergeant. "Rub some powder on your foot. Protects against moisture. It will help."

The sergeant nodded and opened the tin. He poured talc powder on his reddened foot and worked it in as Private Taylor limped back over to his original position.

The sergeant tossed the tin back to the German a few minutes later.

"Do you have extra socks?" The German asked him.

"One pair."

"I'd suggest you put them on. Hang the used ones out to dry or tuck them under your shirt to dry. You've got trench foot symptoms. They're mild, but things will get worse if you don't take care of your foot. Much worse. Dry socks are the best remedy. Change your socks every chance you get."

The sergeant removed a fresh sock from a pocket in his field jacket. He kept an eye on the German as he put the sock on his left foot and laced up his boot. The German's rifle was still on the ground beside him within easy reach, its muzzle pointed at the Americans.

As the afternoon wore on, the German slowly opened up. He told the Americans his name was Helmut. He talked of extensive Allied bombing over Berlin—where his family resided. He also talked somberly about the travails of the German foot soldier. Helmut told them how he had obtained water by melting ice in his helmet, and he talked of foraging for food for days at a time when rations had not been delivered to those on the front lines. He also mentioned fuel shortages and extensive casualties.

The Americans learned that Helmut had been drafted into Germany's recently-created Volkssturm militia which was comprised primarily of teenagers and older men—males who had previously been deemed unfit for combat.

Helmut mentioned that he had a wife and three kids whom he hadn't communicated with for six months. He did not know if they were okay and worried constantly about them, given the Allied bombing over Berlin.

The Americans slowly let their guard down as the afternoon waned. The old German did not appear to be a significant threat. He looked sleep-deprived and defeated, in fact. It did not appear that the man was in any hurry to rejoin his unit.

Late that afternoon, Helmut reached into his coat pocket and extracted three small rectangular pieces of tin. From another pocket he removed a small pair of tin snips and a miniature pair of pliers.

Each piece of tin was roughly the size of a pack of Lucky Strikes. The Americans watched as Helmut cut, bent, and shaped the tin into what appeared to be ornaments—bell-shaped Christmas ornaments.

"I've been working on these as time permits," Helmut announced in his subtle tone. "One for each of my children...I was a metal smith before *this* war. I was teaching my oldest boy the craft just before I was drafted into the Volkssturm."

Helmut finished shaping the last ornament just before sundown. Then he placed the ornaments and hand tools back in his jacket pocket. After that, he reached into his rucksack and extracted a cured sausage.

"I've been saving this for Christmas," he said. "But who knows what tomorrow will bring." Helmut pulled out his pocketknife and cut the meat into four equal pieces. He tossed a piece to each American.

*****

As nightfall approached, the Americans huddled in the bomb crater. The temperature plummeted when the sun went down. A fire was out of the question.

Shortly after sunset, they heard distant singing emanating from the woods north of their position. *Stille Nacht, heilige Nacht...*

Though the Americans didn't speak German, they recognized the song. What they didn't know was whether the Germans singing the carol were from a small patrol—or a much larger unit.

A thoughtful look crossed Helmut's face just then. "I am reminded of the Christmas Truce," he whispered. "It started out much the same—with singing."

"The Christmas Truce?" This from Private Taylor.

"Yes. It took place during the first war."

Sergeant Maclean's eyebrows lifted. "Never heard of it."

"Most people haven't," Helmut acknowledged. "It wasn't authorized by the high command on either side. The Christmas Truce was the doing of soldiers in the trenches."

"My father fought in the Great War," Private Rigby put in. "He never mentioned anything about a Christmas Truce."

"It took place before America entered the war. The year was 1914. My unit had just moved up to the forward trench."

"Where did this truce take place?" Sergeant Maclean inquired.

"On the Western Front. In No Man's Land—the strip of land between the German trenches and the English trenches. There was a ceasefire. Some of our soldiers started to sing carols. Then we heard caroling emanating from the English trenches, too. A few of our soldiers eventually climbed out from our trenches and hesitantly stepped into No Man's Land. Some English soldiers stepped out from their trenches as well. There was no shooting.

181

"After a while, more soldiers from each side left the trenches and ventured out into No Man's Land. This was during daylight, mind you. Some of us actually exchanged gifts with the English."

"Gifts?"

"Yes. The English gave us pipe tobacco. We gave them cigars. There was some exchange of cigarettes and chocolate, too. Those of us that spoke English translated for our comrades that didn't. A game of football broke out not far from our sector if you can believe it... Perhaps someday the children of future generations will read about the Christmas Truce in history books."

*****

The moon was three quarters full. The nightscape was illuminated. The time had come to part company with Helmut. Just a hundred yards south of the bomb crater lay the woods the Americans had attempted to reach earlier that day before all hell broke loose.

Sergeant Maclean glanced up at the night sky. Private Rigby and Private Taylor were beside him. Helmut was removing a pair of socks from his rucksack. It was the moment the sergeant had been waiting for. "Get ready," he whispered to the privates. "The next time cloud cover obscures the moon, I'll give the signal—"

The sudden rumbling of diesel engines shattered the silence. The sergeant motioned for the privates to stay put. Then he made his way up the side of the bomb crater and peered over the edge. The sergeant's heart raced when he saw the enemy convoy break through the woods along the northern edge of the field…The convoy was headed down the field in their direction.

A tracked armored scout vehicle led a long column of halftracks and armored trucks. Behind the column was a wave of Wehrmacht troops.

Sergeant Maclean slipped back down to the bottom of the crater. A few minutes later, they heard German voices. A small patrol of forward observers.

At that moment, Helmut picked up his Mauser and pointed it at the Americans. "Do as I say," he instructed. "Raise your hands above your head."

The Americans had no choice. They'd be easy targets in the moonlit snow-covered field, should they attempt to make a run for the woods. The three of them raised their hands over their heads.

"Now, move out single file," Helmut commanded.

The Americans made their way out of the bomb crater with their hands up. Helmut was behind them, his Mauser trained on their backs. Helmut marched the Americans northward—toward the advancing column.

"Halt!" The voice came from an officer in the scout vehicle at the head of the column. The entire column ground to a stop as Helmut and the three American prisoners neared.

The officer motioned to the soldiers in the halftrack behind the scout vehicle. *"Aussteigen." Disembark.*

Nine Germans disembarked from the halftrack and advanced toward the Americans. Each enemy soldier carried a Mauser rifle. They faced the Americans in a semi-circle formation, their rifles pointed at them.

"Schicken Sie sie," the officer instructed. *Dispatch them.*

Helmut stepped between the Americans and the nine German soldiers.

"Ich glaube nicht, dass das sehr klug wäre," he shouted. *I don't think that would be wise.*

The officer's face reddened. *"Gehen Sie zur Seite."* *Step aside.*

Helmut remained steadfast.

"Dies ist nicht die Zeit, Gefangene zu neehmen!" the officer shouted. *This is not a time to take prisoners!*

There was more dialogue between Helmut and the frustrated officer. It seemed Helmut was attempting to reason with the officer, but the man wasn't buying it. The nine German troops edged closer to the Americans. Then the officer barked out a command. Three of the enemy soldiers approached the Americans. Each one held a length of rope.

"What're they doing, Sarge?" Private Rigby asked. The kid was shaking.

"Don't know."

The three German soldiers bound the Americans' hands behind their backs with rope. Then the irate officer removed his hat and raked his hand through his hair. The Americans thought it was the end, thought they were going to be executed…, but then the officer waved his hand in a dismissive gesture. *"Sehr gut."* *Very well.*

Helmut nodded.

Then the officer said, *"Schaffen Sie die Genfangenen aus unserem Weg."* *Move your prisoners out of our way.*

The nine German soldiers returned to the halftrack as Helmut prodded the Americans with the muzzle of his Mauser and directed them off to the side, away from the column. The Americans exhaled as the nine German soldiers climbed onto the halftrack.

"Then the officer shouted, *"Vorwärts!"* Forward!

As the convoy pulled forward, a wave of JU 88s—Luftwaffe—flew overhead. The explosions from the bombs they dropped over Bastogne minutes later were muffled by the column's halftracks and armored trucks.

Helmut prodded the American's with the muzzle of his Mauser and marched them northward until the convoy and the last of Wehrmacht troops were no longer in sight.

The Americans' hands were still tied behind their backs when Helmut told them to stop. Helmut removed a knife from his belt and approached Sergeant Maclean. Rigby and Taylor watched as Helmut approached the sergeant from behind, raised his knife… and cut the rope that bound the sergeant's wrists. Then he made his way over to Rigby and Taylor. He cut the ropes that bound their hands, too.

"What did you tell that officer?" the sergeant asked Helmut.

"I told him I felt that dispatching the three of you would be a mistake. I informed him that your knowledge of recent American troop movement would surely be of interest to the high command. I told him I was on my way to the rear to bring you three in for interrogation."

The sergeant nodded.

"This is where we must part company, comrades," Helmut announced. "Do any of you have a compass?"

"Yes," Sergeant Maclean replied.

"Good. You probably already know that the American line is due south of here."

The sergeant nodded once more. "Yes."

Private Rigby reached into his rucksack and extracted a Hershey Bar. He handed it to Helmut.

Helmut's eyes widened. "I can't recall the last time I had chocolate. Thank you."

Private Taylor removed a K-ration from his rucksack and handed it to Helmut. "It's nothing like that sausage, but it's all I have to give you. Happy holidays."

"And to you. Thank you." Helmut placed the Hersey bar and the K-ration in his rucksack.

Sergeant Maclean didn't have a Hershey Bar or even a K-ration to offer Helmut. But he did have a pad of paper and a pen in his rucksack. He reached into his rucksack and removed them. Then he ripped off a sheet a sheet of paper from the pad and penned a note.

December 24, 1944

To Whom it May Concern:

This German soldier saved the lives of three Americans. Please treat him with respect.

Sincerely,

Sergeant Gerald Maclean
101ˢᵗ Airborne Division

Sergeant Maclean handed the note to the Helmut. "If you're captured, give this to an American officer."

Helmut nodded. "Thank you." Then he reached into his coat pocket and removed the three bell-shaped ornaments. "It looks like I won't be making it home for Christmas this year," he said. He handed each American an ornament. "*Frohe Weihnachten*—Merry Christmas."

"Merry Christmas, Helmut."

The Americans pocketed the ornaments. Then they bid Helmut farewell and headed south across the moonlit field.

Later that night, after they had retrieved their carbines and were deep in the woods trying to find their way back to their unit, they heard a most remarkable sound: church bells. Somehow, a church was still intact after all of the bombing, shelling, and small arms fire. It had survived. And the three Americans would, too.

Chapter 30

My grandfather's eyes were watery as he concluded his story. A few moments passed in silence after he finished talking. Then he slowly reached into the small wooden box on the coffee table and removed the object wrapped in white tissue paper.

All eyes were on him as he slowly peeled the tissue paper away…and revealed a bell-shaped tin ornament. My grandfather held it up for all to see.

Unlike the crystal star, it was a simple ornament, but it was apparent that it had been crafted an artisan. The bell was symmetrical, and the bottom was perfectly flared. There was even a small loop at the top for a ribbon. One would never guess that the ornament had been crafted on a battlefield.

My grandfather handed the ornament to my mother. She studied the ornament for a while and handed it to my father. The ornament was passed around the room from person to person.

"Did you ever see Helmut again?" I asked my grandfather.

"No. Our paths never crossed again…He gifted us with so much— food, medical attention, kinship. The man saved our lives. But I had nothing to give him…I wish the circumstances could have been different. I always wished I could have repaid him somehow."

My father put his hand on my grandfather's shoulder. "You did give Helmut something, Dad. You gave him the letter. That letter you wrote for him was a true gift. I'm sure it gave Helmut hope. And it very well may have saved his life."

A slow smile creased my grandfather's face. "Thanks, Son. I guess I never looked at it like that. Who knows? Perhaps you're right."

I was the last person to hold the tin bell-shaped ornament. The lights on the Christmas tree reflected off the tin ornament as I admired it. It was truly unique. In my hand was a piece of history.

I attempted to hand the ornament back to my grandfather a few minutes later, but he held his hands up in refusal. "You keep it," he said "for your Christmas Tin."

"Are you sure?"

"Yes, it's time I passed it along."

"Thank you."

"Don't mention it...I'll be right back."

My grandfather got up and left the room. When he returned a few minutes later, he was carrying an old scrapbook. He set the scrapbook down on the coffee table. "This might be of interest."

Everyone gathered around my grandfather as he opened the scrapbook. The first few pages contained old articles from *Stars & Stripes*. Pasted to the next three pages were mementos: letters from my grandmother, a 101st Airborne Division patch, a USO show advertisement, a WWII ration stamp, a telegram.

My grandfather took his time as he thumbed through the scrapbook. He talked about the history of the 101st Airborne Division patch. And he mentioned seeing Marlene Dietrich perform at a USO show.

There were several pages of photographs in the scrapbook, too. One photograph was of two young soldiers in a foxhole at the edge of a snow-crusted field. "Private Taylor is the one on the left. That's Rigby beside him. Never saw anyone that could put food away like that kid."

On the next page was a photograph of a young blonde-haired sergeant in front of a jeep. My grandfather. How confident and proud he looked.

In another photograph, a dozen weary-looking soldiers attended Mass in a church that had been bombed. Half of the church's roof was missing.

There was also a photograph of liberated Dutch civilians cheering a group of American soldiers. "That one was taken in Holland," my grandfather stated.

There were other photographs as well. Photographs of bazooka teams positioned at the edges of snow-covered fields; soldiers manning .50 caliber machine guns; a GI opening a K-ration in front of a camouflaged tank.

The men in the photographs looked cold and tired. I was still thinking about them when I turned in later that night and pulled up the covers. How lucky I was to have a roof overhead and a warm bed to sleep in.

Epilogue
December 24, 2010

The logs in the fireplace had been reduced to embers when I concluded. Anna stared into the fireplace. It seemed as if she was mesmerized by the orange glow of the embers, but I suspected she was processing everything she'd just heard. A few moments later she turned and looked at me.

"Wow, Dad. I had *no* idea about your situation last year," she said. "I'm so sorry you had to go through all that."

"Thanks, kiddo. But everything worked out for the best. In retrospect, I'm glad I went through what I did. I wouldn't be where I am today if Central New England Real Estate Group hadn't laid me off."

"You are the master of keeping secrets."

I grinned. "You got me there."

"So, the new business is going well?"

I nodded. "I'm glad to report that it is. Better than expected, actually. We assumed the management of two new apartment complexes last month. And we recently diversified into brokerage."

"That's fantastic!"

"Thanks. I feel very fortunate."

"What about Wendy? Did she find a new job?"

"She did. Wendy is our vice president. She's doing quite well, just bought a new townhouse in a development we manage across town."

"Good for her! She deserves it."

"She does indeed."

"And how about Jaimes O'Malluy? Was he upset when you quit?"

I smiled. "No, on the contrary. Jaimes O'Malluy is a business partner now. We're developing a small lot across town. Jaimes is the builder."

"A happy ending all around."

"Yes indeed."

The Christmas Tin was on the coffee table in front of us. Anna leaned forward and peered into it. Then she extracted the three ornaments that had been placed in the tin last December—a crystal star, a paper angel, and a tin bell. Anna set the ornaments down gently on the coffee table.

A few moments passed in comfortable silence as we admired the ornaments. Then Anna said, "You know, Dad, you really ought to write this stuff down—the stories behind the gifts in the Christmas Tin. I've read some of the pieces you wrote during your days as a correspondent. You know how to tell a story. I think people would be interested to hear the stories behind the gifts in the Christmas Tin—especially around the holidays."

My eyebrows lifted. "I've been pretty busy lately, but I'll give it some thought."

*****

That night, when everyone else in the house was asleep, I took my laptop downstairs to the kitchen table. I poured a glass of eggnog and placed half a dozen Christmas cookies on a plate. Then I placed the eggnog and cookies on the table. After that, I sat down and turned on my laptop.

As I waited for the laptop to boot up, I flashed back to the previous fall when I had sat at that same table, frantically searching for a job. How things had changed. This time, when my laptop booted up, rather than log on to the Internet to search for a job, I opened up a new Microsoft Word document and started to type.

As with the stories I wrote during my days as a correspondent, I began with the title. At the top of page, I typed... *The Christmas Tin.*